NAZIR
THE WHITE FIRE

Philip Antony

Cover Illustration by Mackenzie Rose Ridgeway

For my beloved Sara Jean –

My editor, best friend, and soul mate

Acknowledgements

It is with enormous gratitude mixed with sadness that I acknowledge the invaluable contribution of Sara Jean who was my first and most critical editor; who helped me with the numerous rewrites, and most importantly, offered suggestions and comments that made this story come alive. She gave me the encouragement to continue to write not only this story but also many others. Sadly, she is no longer with me, and will be sorely missed as my best advisor, truest friend and life partner.

CONTENTS

GLOSSARY

1. **Zoltan:** the greatest of the gods. He is the creator of the universe, father of the Goddess of Earth, Amira, and brother to the witch goddess Haroda.

2. **Amira:** the Goddess of Earth

3. The **Age of Harat**: the time that began with the birth of the goddess Amira.

4. **Azurat:** the Blue Stone of Creation. The stone contains the energy that powers the four elements: Earth, Air, Fire, and Water. The Azurat Stone hangs from Amira's neck. She and the stone are one – each requires the other.

5. **Wadiri:** the desert garden; birthplace of the Earth Goddess, Amira. The Wadiri is hidden from all but the gods and is protected by the Azurat stone.

6. **Haroda:** the Goddess of the Underworld and the sister of Zoltan. She has dominion over the evil

creatures and beasts that reside there. She stole the power to make the Earth shake and to cause volcanoes to erupt. For that, her brother, Zoltan, banished her to the Underworld. Prior to her violation, she was the most beautiful of the gods, but now she is hideous to look at.

7. **Galthoram:** the Underworld, ruled by the Guardian of the Underworld, Haroda. Those who committed evil in the world were condemned here for all eternity. Once condemned, there was no return.

8. **Makor:** the God of the Volcanoes, who kept the continents in place; he harnessed the power of the Earth's molten core from which iron and gold sprang. He was rendered powerless by Haroda, who stole his power. He was now a shell who sat in an empty chamber in Galthoram, staring into the distance.

9. **Loganne:** the great and powerful wolf pack leader, who was appointed by Amira to be the leader of the

other creatures. It is Loganne who is responsible for ensuring that the creatures of the forest remain true to their natures and loyal to the Earth Goddess, Amira.

10. **Zunir:** the Land of Forgotten Souls. Haroda imprisons mortals here. The punishment in the Zunir is not fire or ice, but the loss of all hope forever. The pain of loss from ever being freed from this place is unbearable.

11. **Gaius Fortus:** a magician who succumbed to the deception of Haroda, who promised to make him the Greatest of Wizards, but then reneged on her promise and imprisoned him in the Zunir. He was a kindly man whose salvation lies in teaching Nazir the ways of the White Fire. He rescued Jamila and the other children from imprisonment by Haroda, who imprisoned him because he dared to defy the witch. Only the White Fire can free him.

12. **Lashot:** the tormentor of souls in the Cave of Sorrows. Lashot was a cruel, dark spirit who punished the condemned by eating them and, after spitting them out, devoured them again – over and over for all eternity. The only way past Lashot was to possess an absolutely pure and blameless spirit.

13. The **Craxon:** a dark spirit that inhabited the desert and manifested itself in the form of a dragon composed of desert sand. The sand dragon was commanded by Haroda.

14. **Volarian Warlocks:** dreaded creatures who had the power to conjure evil. This was the army at the command of the witch Haroda. These horrible creatures were neither body nor spirit but manifestations of Haroda's evil. They possessed physical power; and they could inflict terrible emotional harm on their victims.

15. **Jabhar:** a village in the middle of the vast desert. Home of the Karash people. Once nomads

themselves, they settled to provide comfort to the wandering tribes and to trade. The village was ravaged by Haroda's magic

16. **Jamila**: daughter to Sha Ram leader of the village of Jabhar. She was the only person who knew the location of the entrance to Galthoram.

17. The **Siwa:** a large black falcon that flew at the command of Haroda to prey upon the innocent people loyal to Zoltan. It was a merciless killer. The Siwa had the power to replicate itself into thousands and could destroy an entire army. The Siwa's wing span was 20 feet across and it stood 20 feet in height.

18. **Ricon**: a serpent and the vilest and most dangerous of all the inhabitants of Galthoram. It resided in the deepest pit of the hell that was Galthoram – the Lake of Eternal Fire. Even Haroda feared this monster.

CHAPTER 1

The Age of Harat

From the first moment he gazed upon her, Zoltan – the greatest of the gods and Creator of the Universe – proclaimed that she was the most beautiful of all his children. She would enjoy his special favor and protection. He did love them all, but this child, Amira, was his favorite. He doted over her like no other. Her eyes were like little blue crystals – deep, warm and gentle. Amira followed Zoltan's every movement and searched the sky when he was not within her immediate sight. It was only for him that she would smile, and when she did, she warmed his heart to bursting. He knew that this child would be the greatest of his creations. She was endowed with abiding love, compassion and intellect.

Zoltan searched the universe for a special place for the baby goddess to live. Finally, he came upon a little blue-green planet called Earth. So beautiful was this little pearl suspended in the dark expanse of the universe that he decided there and then that this should be the place for Amira. Here she would grow and flourish alongside the dwellers of the planet: humankind. He also saw that this place, beautiful as it was, could also be unpredictable, hostile, and dangerous. Both the people and the land itself were often in upheaval. The various tribes were constantly at war, fighting over trivialities that they had made monumentally important in order to justify the sacrifices necessary to win. However, there were never really any winners; nothing was ever resolved. Both sides of the conflict suffered untold hardship falling mostly on innocent people who wanted nothing more than to live in peace. What remained was only remorseless death and suffering, which was all too soon forgotten.

The planet's environment was also given to violence. There were savage storms, earthquakes that shook the land, and devastating volcanoes that produced rivers of molten fire, annihilating everything in its path. Still, Zoltan marveled at the raw beauty of this place. He would entrust this jewel of a planet into Amira's hands. She would be its protector; she would fashion it in her image: beauty, wonder and promise. She was anointed the Goddess of Earth.

Thus began the **Age of Harat**.

With a wave of his arm, Zoltan transformed a desert valley that once was arid and desolate into a lush and verdant paradise. The burning sand and stones were replaced with magnificent palms, bubbling springs and a carpet of green grass to provide a bed for his child goddess. She was adorned with white, blue and yellow flowers that charged the air around her with sweet, hypnotic fragrances. To feed his precious gift, Zoltan created tangles of shrubs and trees that were weighed down with figs, dates and apricots. Grapes hung from vines, and olives grew with abandon. Bees provided a constant supply of honey. Water burst out from the depths to bathe her. The sun warmed her and the stars were strewn about in the night sky to keep her amused.

As a sign to all creation that Amira enjoyed Zoltan's special favor and protection, he fashioned a special crystal from the blue of the sky and the raw power of the sun that warmed the Earth. He endowed the crystal with power over all natural things on this beautiful planet. This magnificent and powerful gem was the Azurat – the Blue Stone of Creation. There was no gemstone like it in the entire universe. As he placed the jewel around the child's neck, he commanded, "Whoever shall wear this stone shall have my power over the earth and all its inhabitants."

It instantly glowed as bright as the morning sun, and as deep as the night sky. He bent over and placed his hand on her forehead; it had the effect of fusing the stone and the child forever. The fate of the stone would now be her fate. To protect his special child until she grew to womanhood, Zoltan threw a blue cloak over the entire valley rendering it invisible and impenetrable. The valley instantly disappeared. The ancient ones called it the Wadiri, the 'desert garden.'

For a thousand years, Amira grew from a child to a woman. Her beauty was like a glorious morning sun and as simple as a daisy flower. She had the beauty of a butterfly that skipped from flower to flower. She was as flawless as the Azurat gem that hung from her neck. The Earth absorbed her breath; she exhaled its energy and beauty. She had become the Earth itself from which all things would flow. She possessed the power of the Earth, the life-giving force from which all life must spring.

Her companions were the creatures of the forest, the trees, the brook, birds and the flowers – each spoke to her in their own language, and in turn, she protected and nurtured them. They taught her to fly, to sing and to speak the languages of the Earth, the wind, the sky and the water. The trees whispered to her; flowers giggled with her; fish taught her to swim. Her laughter was carried by the wind and filled the secret valley. Her childhood was filled with happiness and undisturbed freedom. Zoltan charged Logane, the most powerful of wolves, with the responsibility for the safety of Amira and the creatures of the Wadiri. He was Amira's most loyal guardian and friend.

Although he was the greatest of the gods, Zoltan was powerless to prevent petty jealousies and strife among the other lesser gods. Equally, it was an all too similar issue for the mortals who inhabited the Earth, the home of his child, the Earth Goddess, Amira. It saddened him to see that the Immortals, the gods of the Unending Universe, could squabble and whine just like the inhabitants of the Earth over such trivialities as power, influence, and their place in the hierarchy of gods. It was a pernicious problem that threatened the order and stability of the universe, and if unchecked, could prove destructive to everyone and everything in the cosmos.

The other gods quickly learned of the birth of the child Amira, and Zoltan's unabashed feelings for her, and his unconcealed favoritism. Most would not dare to challenge or criticize Zoltan, except for the Goddess Haroda, Zoltan's sister and now Guardian of the Underworld – the Galthoram. It was in this place that those who had committed evil in the world above were condemned for all eternity. Once condemned, there was no return. Haroda's minions were the evil creatures and beasts that tormented and tortured the condemned. They obeyed her every command.

Haroda had been banished by Zoltan at an earlier age for abducting Makor, the God of the Volcanoes, and holding him hostage for 1,000 years. It was

Makor who kept the continents in place and harnessed the power of the Earth's molten core from which iron and gold sprang. She released him only after Zoltan himself came to his rescue, but not before Haroda had stolen Makor's power to make fire and shake the Earth. The witch, by then, had reduced Makor to a shell. She left him with only the memories of his former glory. He now sat alone in an empty chamber, silently staring into the distance, tortured for an eternity. Such was her cruelty. Now, Haroda possessed the power, and it was from the depths of Galthoram that the evil witch could make mountains explode, cause rivers of fire to engulf, and destroy everything in its path.

"Zoltan, you claim to be the greatest of the gods, yet you dote over this child like a hapless dog drooling over a piece of meat. What is she that she deserves such favor? And why have you given her dominion over the Earth?" demanded Haroda.

"Silence!" Zoltan bellowed to Haroda. "Yours is not to question. I am the greatest of the gods, and it is I, and only I who commands the universe, who dispenses life and whatever favor I choose. I have chosen this child because of her purity of spirit, goodness of heart, and compassion that extends to all creatures. I have spoken. It shall be so."

Haroda was unbowed. He may be the greatest of the gods, she thought, but he held no sway in the dark regions of Galthoram – the Underworld. This was her domain. The Underworld was a forbidding and noxious place. The air was foul, and the putrid smell of death hung throughout. There were both extremes of ice and fire – furiously mixing together in this hellish cauldron. Her rule in this kingdom of the damned was harsh and cruel. As pure, good and compassionate as the young goddess Amira was, Haroda was her antithesis. Once condemned to Galthoram, there was no reprieve or escape. However, the greatest pain suffered by the damned was not punishment and pain, but rather the loss of hope.

Haroda herself was as ugly as a beast. Her features were distorted and gnarled, owing not so much to age but rather to the venom that flowed in her veins. Her skin was a dull green and slimy, pockmarked with black and blue. She had the eyes of the dreaded black cobra – bright orange, cold and deadly. Her mottled hair fell to her waist in a tangled, knotted mass from which hung large worms. Her mouth was permanently twisted in the shape of a snarl from which large fang-like teeth protruded. A black cape covered her misshapen body that was stooped over. Indeed, she resembled the hooded, black cobra.

Zoltan roared, "Leave witch; return to the deep pit from which you have emerged. Go back to your misery and torment."

Haroda turned to leave, and then stopped and turned to face Zoltan, "You will regret this, Zoltan.

You may call yourself the greatest of the gods, but you have become weak and soft. The Earth must be ruled with strength and absolute power, not by an old man coddling a child. It is I who should rule over the Earth – not you. It is I who should have dominion over all earthly creation."

With that, Haroda flew from the Great Chamber into the depths, screaming curses and abuse. It was then that she vowed to take revenge on Zoltan for condemning her to Galthoram, for taking away her former beauty, and for anointing Amira with dominion over the Earth instead of her. She would take what was rightfully hers: domination of the Earth. She knew she could not overpower the great king and his armies, but she had to find another way to bring him to his knees. There was no need to engage her legions of the damned in a losing battle with Zoltan. Her plan was simple: destroy Amira, and take possession of the Azurat, whatever the cost.

Deep in her hellish chamber in Galthoram, she pondered all the possibilities; she consulted all the evil forces over which she had dominion. None could find a way to defeat Zoltan, or to penetrate the Wadiri. Oh, yes, the gods knew where the Wadiri was. However, none but Haroda would dare to attempt to breach the blue veil. For ten thousand years, Haroda tried, but every attempt of hers failed. Rather than discouraging her, her failures fueled her anger and determination even more, to destroy the Wadiri, overpower the Earth Goddess Amira, to dominate the Earth, and in so doing, achieve her ultimate goal: the destruction of Zoltan.

In the middle of the eternal night, as the fires and ice of Galthoram consumed the doomed souls, it came to her. Why hadn't she thought of this before? "For thousands of years, it has eluded me. But, the answer is here; here in Galthoram!" she screeched in delight. "If I cannot penetrate the Wadiri from above, I shall invade it from beneath." How simple!

No one could possibly suspect. And so, her plan began to unfold.

She summoned up the power of the volcanoes that she had stolen from Makor and, with a wave of her crooked arm, sent a tremor up from the bowels of Galthoram into the Wadiri, the desert garden.

It was in the late afternoon; Amira was seated in the middle of a field, playing with butterflies and laughing at the antics of a flock of crows. As she was about to take flight to join them, the ground underneath her began to sway, slowly at first, and then it started shaking more violently. The Earth first groaned as if in pain and then roared in agony. Suddenly, large cracks opened up in the Earth from which fountains of fire gushed high in the air. It seemed as if the Earth was being torn apart. She was thrown to her knees, but quickly covered herself with her stole to shield herself from the black ash that was pouring out of the once-blue sky of the Earth. She summoned her power over the Earth to command this torment to stop – but to no avail. This was a power she had never experienced. Was this a natural phenomenon, she thought, or the work of other sinister forces? Within moments, the sun disappeared behind clouds of dust and ash; and the sky turned from blue to red as plumes of fire filled the air.

Amira called out to the birds, "Fly high, fly high!"

She then called out to the other creatures in the Wadiri, "Flee, my children, run from here. I am powerless to save you. Go, quickly!"

The great wolf, Logane, spoke first, "No, my queen, we will not abandon you. If this is the work of dark forces, we will stay and fight with you to the end."

Despite the cacophony and fire surrounding Amira and Logane, the goddess knelt down in front of the wolf pack leader, and said gently, "You are the bravest of the brave, my dear Logane, but I fear there are forces at work here that are beyond us. Save yourself and the others. I wear the Azurat; Zoltan protects me. No harm can come to me."

Logane looked at her for a long time, hoping she would change her mind, but Amira's only thought was for her beloved children, the living things of the Wadiri. The wolf bowed his head, "Yes, my queen." He then disappeared into the forest, calling as he did to the other beings to follow him.

For the first time, Amira, Goddess of the Earth, was now alone. The magnificent trees were consumed in fire, the flowers disappeared, and the streams and brooks dried up. She searched the burning sky for an intruder who may have caused this devastation. Suddenly the Earth erupted in front of her with an explosion that created a massive fireball from which emerged the wicked Haroda, Goddess of the Underworld, Galthoram.

"Amira, Goddess of the Earth; Queen of all its inhabitants. Ha! You are nothing before me. You are like these simple creatures you call your friends, your children. They are insignificant, and you, like them, are expendable. I will destroy them, and destroy you."

Amira was stunned. She could not believe that this was the work of one of the gods. She had always thought of them as benevolent. True, they were not all perfect, but she could not imagine that anyone was capable of such monstrous treachery.

"Haroda, why, why are you doing this? These humble creatures...we mean you no harm," Amira stumbled over her words, so great was her shock.

The witch screamed her response. "Why? Why? Because you are Zoltan's favorite; because he has bestowed this Earth on you; because this Earth should be my dominion; and mostly because I hate him, I loathe him. There shall be no mercy."

She decided that rather than killing Amira, she would hurt Zoltan more by destroying the valley, and taking the Azurat, which would render Amira helpless and as insignificant as the most pitiful of creatures of the Wadiri.

She summoned her legion of the damned, which formed a ring around Amira, a ring of evil and terror. These creatures were even more hideous than Haroda. These revolting beasts resembled a black, shapeless gelatinous mold; some had eyes, some did not; several had limbs like an octopus with razor-sharp claws, while there were some with long fangs protruding at different angles. But they did have one thing in common: they emitted the suffocating stench of death and decay. Their combined shrieks were louder and more piercing than the loudest thunder. On the witch's command, they attacked the Earth Goddess with all their fury. Amira fought the forces of this evil army with all her might, but for as many as she slew, Haroda summoned more. The battle raged unabated for days.

Haroda knew that as long as the Earth Goddess wore the Azurat, she would not succumb, but if the

Azurat were to fall from Amira's neck, the battle would be lost, and Haroda would be the victor. Haroda raised her twisted arm and screamed, "***Alga seech borano,***" which instantly caused the Earth under Amira's feet to split open, revealing the black abyss of Galthoram. Amira plummeted into the pit, and as she did so, Haroda swept in and tore the Azurat from Amira's neck. As she was falling, Amira tried to call out to Zoltan, but the screaming legions drowned out her voice. The beautiful Goddess of the Earth was swallowed up, and then disappeared as Haroda closed the dark pit over her.

In that instant, the Wadiri – Zoltan's bucolic desert garden – home to Amira, Goddess of Earth and all its creatures – was transformed back to a bleak and desolate valley. The brutal sun burned the stones, and the hot wind blew the sand across the arid plain. The creatures of the valley disappeared. All that was left was death and misery.

CHAPTER 2

Nazir, the Desert Boy

"Nazir, Nazir, where are you? I need you to fetch some water," the woman called out, turning her head over her shoulder.

"Yes, Mother," the boy replied.

He dutifully picked up the bucket to walk several miles to the oasis. As he stepped out of his family's tent, Nazir stopped and shielded his eyes from the sun with one hand on his forehead to see the vast expanse of the desert in the distance where the deep blue of the sky melted into the tan of the sand and the reddish mountains at the horizon. He never got tired of this breathtaking view. For all its harshness, he loved the desert. It was beautiful, eerily silent, and also forbidding. It was home.

The desert has its own rhythm, and he and his tribe moved in concert with it. Nazir took a deep breath to inhale the dry, still air. He closed his eyes and held his breath for a moment savoring the warmth that filled his lungs. He wrapped the scarf around his head and mouth, leaving only his eyes exposed, and then set off. He looked over his shoulder to see his mother and waved her goodbye. She lifted her hand hesitantly to return his gesture. She continued to watch him as he made his way down the path until he disappeared behind a dune.

Nazir was born in a tent in the desert, the only child in his family that belonged to a tribe of nomad people. His father had died when Nazir was a very young boy, but his memories of him were very much alive. He remembered the wooden sword he had given him and the days when father and son practiced in mock combat. Those were happy days. The little boy would swing his sword and chase his father round and round the tent, and then switch, with father chasing son – both laughing while his mother watched these antics, shaking her head and smiling.

"I don't know which one of you is the child. You should stop before you hurt yourself," she said to her panting husband, who was doubled over, breathless and dizzy, chasing the boy who seemed to have an endless well of energy. Nazir clung to these few memories of his father – he still had the wooden sword, which he kept wrapped in a blanket by his sleeping mat.

His mother, Lara, taught Nazir to read and write. She had also taught him his numbers. More importantly, she taught him love, compassion and truth – and she did this by example. However, what he remembered most of his life was its tranquility and peace. In the quiet moments of the night when all of the members of the tribe were asleep, he would sit outside his tent to look into the night sky, where a full moon cast eerie shadows over the dunes, and stars sprinkled across the sky like seeds. It was the silence and solitude that he enjoyed most of all – the quiet time when he was alone with the desert and the sky. This was the time he spoke to his father about his daily triumphs and the emptiness he felt without him. Yes, he loved his mother dearly, but he longed for the days when he would sit with his father at night gazing into the heavens, searching for the star patterns his father had taught him. "There, Nazir, do you see it? That is the Archer constellation. And there is the North Star, your guide, should you ever be lost in the desert. Find it, and you will find your home."

One day, as his father lay dying in his tent, he summoned his young son to his side. "Nazir, my beloved son. The God of gods has called me. I shall be gone soon, but I shall always be with you. Look into the night sky; look to the stars – I shall be among them. I will always be there for you. Be strong, my son. You must look after your mother."

Suddenly, it became very quiet. It seemed as if the Earth and everything in it had stopped. The man reached out for his son's hand and looked at the young boy for the last time as his lips whispered, "I love you." His eyes remained fixed on his son even after his last breath. Since then, he and his mother had struggled, but with the help of the others in his tribe, they managed.

The people of the desert possessed the rugged good looks of those who had lived for ages under the sun - dark-skinned with dark hair and deep, dark penetrating eyes. The nomads were traders, and the men of the tribe were expected to be strong, fearless, cunning, and, when necessary, fierce fighters. However, this was not Nazir. Nazir was handsome, taller than the other children, but very slightly built. He was quiet, studious, and introspective. He was also generous with his time, especially with little children. He taught them about reading and mathematics, the desert, the night sky and the stars.

The little children followed him incessantly, asking him for help or questions to which he happily obliged. In honor of his father, he tried to compete in the games required of the young men who aspired to take their places among the men around the council fires. This was the dream for every boy, but it was not to be for Nazir. He had tried to live up to the dream of his father to be a warrior-leader of the tribe, but for all his attempts to follow in his father's path, it became clearer to him, his mother, and especially the other members of the tribe that this young boy was not a warrior, but somehow different.

"I don't understand, mother. I have tried to learn the ways of the desert warriors. I have practiced with the knife and sword, but I have not achieved much more than when I played with Father. I am defeated in every combat. Why, mother? Why can't I be like the others? What is wrong with me?"

She sensed his frustration and anger. Her heart ached for her son. She wanted to tell him that he was different, that he was, in fact, **not** like the others but had other gifts that made him special. He was unique, and because of that, she knew in her heart that he would achieve so much – not through the ways of the warrior but through others yet to be revealed. How could she tell this young boy all those things? She knew that he would not accept it. She put her arms around him, and gently said, "My dear Nazir. I don't know why, but I do believe that there is a larger plan for you. You may indeed be different, but this is for a purpose unknown to both of us."

Nazir was now eighteen years old on the fateful day that he walked into the desert, bucket in hand, to fetch water from the oasis. At the very same time, the elders were meeting around the council fire to speak about the next generation and their readiness to take on the role of leaders. They were satisfied with all of the young men except Nazir.

"What shall we do with him?" asked one of the elders.

"If he cannot protect our tribe, then of what use is he?" said another.

Each of the men, in turn, expressed their doubts about Nazir as a future leader. The current chief of the tribe, Arosh, listened and watched the proceedings intently, eyes squinting as if to penetrate the real thoughts behind each speaker's eyes. He waited for each of the elders to speak. Arosh was a large, muscular man, larger than the others. He had fierce eyes and leathery skin that showed the years in the sun, and the scars from earlier battles with marauding bandits. When all had finished speaking, it was clear that no one had, or would speak in favor of the strange boy, Nazir, in their midst. The council fell silent for a long time. The elders waited for Arosh to speak.

Arosh looked at each member of the council in turn and then spoke slowly, deliberately, "My friends, it is true that the boy will never be a fighter, but let us not forget that he has grown up without a father; he and his mother have struggled. There was no one to show him the ways of the desert warrior. Remember, however, it was Nazir who has taught our younger children to read, and to count. It is he who maintains the accounts of our trades with the other tribes. Are these not contributions that we must take into consideration?" Arosh looked around at the somber faces of the council members.

He then picked up a stick and poked at the waning fire causing the flame to jump. He looked at the end of the glowing stick, and gently blew on it. The glow increased from red to blue to a brilliant white, and then burst into a flame. He spoke again, "Look, my friends, look at this stick. The tip glows bright and hot – we are the fire at this tip, but I tell you, without the remainder of the stick, there could be no fire. Nazir is that stick."

The elders understood; each nodded in affirmation. It was decided that Nazir would be invited to sit at the council fire, but little did they know that such was not to be. It would come to pass that Nazir would be destined for a future that no one in his tribe could have ever imagined.

Suddenly, the wind that was just then beginning to blow harder on the faces of the elders foretold of an extraordinary journey that would bring Nazir out of obscurity to greatness. Arosh lifted his face to the wind. Something was different; something was wrong. The sand stung his face, and as it did, it sent a rush of cold and fear into his heart. He wrapped his scarf across his face. Yes, something was very wrong.

∞

Zoltan proclaimed, "I shall visit my beloved, Amira in the Wadiri."

The gods of water, fire and wind were commanded to join him. Upon their arrival, they immediately realized that the Wadiri had disappeared. Where there was once unimaginable beauty, there was now nothing but a harsh, barren wasteland with its unrelenting heat and waves of burning sand as far as the eyes could see.

Zoltan bellowed his fury. "This is the work of Haroda, the witch of Galthoram!"

Haroda rose out of the depths to meet Zoltan. "Yes, my misguided brother. Your arrogance has brought this about," as she waved her arm around the arid valley. "The other gods bow down to your imperious rule, but not I. It is I, Haroda, who now rules the Earth and all its inhabitants. They will bow to me as the Goddess of the Earth. Amira is no more; it is I who wears the Azurat stone."

His voice was like thunder, "What have you done with her? If any harm befalls her, you will pay dearly for this treachery."

Haroda cackled, "She is safe...for now, but you shall never see her again." With that, Haroda descended into Galthoram, laughing at her evident victory over Zoltan.

Zoltan's anger could not be assuaged. His beloved Amira was now a prisoner in Galthoram, the Azurat stone was around Haroda's neck and the Earth was being subjected to her harsh, vengeful rule. He had to stop her before she could dispose of Amira in the fiery pit of hell. Yes, it was time, time to call upon the only person who could defeat Haroda and bring back Amira and the Azurat, and restore the Earth to its former beauty.

It was time to find the "White Fire."

CHAPTER 3

Haroda, The Witch of Galthoram

In her subterranean chamber, Haroda saw a vision in her troubled sleep. It was of a slight boy who lived with the nomads, a boy who would rise to greatness among mortals, and possess powers to rival hers. She knew that there was a legend of a mortal who had once been endowed by Zoltan with power equal to that of the gods. Such an extraordinary gift had been awarded to a mortal only once in all of the ages since the beginning of time. No mortal since the first one was deserving of such an honor. Although he loved the humans as they were his creation, Zoltan recognized that they were weak, and as a result, were also capable of inhuman behaviors. They could fight with each other, steal, and cheat one another to acquire possessions. They were even capable of killing one another. Yet, he knew that they were also capable of uncommon acts of love, courage and honor. For as horrific as their behaviors could be, they could also demonstrate astonishing acts of generosity and compassion for one another. He had not planned it that way. They had evolved into this mix of opposites and contradictions. It was for this reason that he had anointed one to whom all the mortals could look for inspiration, hope and especially, guidance. This mortal would serve as the role model for all others; and who would serve as a beacon of truth and integrity. Such a person would possess purity of spirit and goodness of heart. He called this mortal the "White Fire." For many years, the White Fire walked among the other mortals who sought his leadership and wise counsel. He was admired and loved by all who came in contact with him. Then one day, without warning, he disappeared and was never heard from again. Some said that he fell under the spell of the evil Haroda. Others said that he succumbed to the weight of the responsibility he carried. It was all too much. The awesome power that he possessed had become an unbearable burden. Over time, the White Fire receded from the memory of the mortals, and so did his example of love, honor and integrity. Without his guidance, humans fell back into their old ways of selfishness, hatred and cruelty to one another.

Zoltan had searched for a thousand years to find another deserving mortal who would serve as his standard bearer, the person who would uphold the rule of law, truth and justice. It had to be a person of virtue, a person without the stain of evil], a person of honor, unfailing courage and a sense of duty. Now, with Amira's kidnapping by Haroda, Zoltan needed urgently to find that person if he were ever to see Amira again.

Then, Zoltan saw the young desert boy, with a bucket in hand, fetching water for his mother. He also saw that this boy, Nazir, possessed all the qualities that Zoltan the Creator wanted in a successor to the White Fire: one who could restore order and balance to the world, and be the example of all that was good in human beings. And, of course, rescue his beloved daughter, Amira. Yes, the time had come...

Haroda saw it in a dream: the White Fire had come again.

Haroda flew into a rage. She knew what it meant. Zoltan had chosen a mortal, one with power equal to the gods, one who would serve as his sword of justice, and who would avenge the atrocities she had committed. He would send the White Fire to rescue Amira, retake the Azurat, and then restore peace and harmony on the Earth.

"Never!" she screamed. "You will not win, Zoltan. I shall slay him just as I destroyed the first White Fire. Yes, Zoltan, it was I that took your first precious White Fire. No mortal shall have power over me. The Azurat is mine; you shall never see Amira again," she shrieked. Her rage would not be calmed until she had destroyed Zoltan's new White Fire. From the depths of Galthoram, she summoned the dark forces at her command, *"Shash delo set, shash delo set."* At that instant, a sandstorm rose up from the desert floor, and became like a veil that shrouded the sun and the sky. The sand was really a monster flying across the desert, choking everything in its path. It had a ferocity never before seen.

∞

Sand and stone were hurled at the nomads, who were helpless to do anything but fall to the ground and cover themselves and each other. Arosh's shout to the other members of the tribe was drowned out by the roar of the monster wind that had been conjured by Haroda. He managed to get the women and the children in a tight cluster and then ordered the men to throw themselves on top of them to shield them from the blistering torrent. Before being buried by the hot, stinging sand, Arosh counted all of the members of the tribe – they were all now safely in the huddle – all but one: Nazir.

∞

Nazir was making his way along the hard path worn by centuries of other nomads trekking to the oasis for water. He was lost in his thoughts when he became overwhelmed with a sense of foreboding. It was a feeling of dread and gloom – he had not felt such things before. It was as if there was a dark force lurking above him. His thoughts were suddenly interrupted. The young boy heard it coming up behind him before he felt the penetrating sting of wind-blown sand in his eyes. He turned, but before he could do anything, a massive wall of sand struck him full force. The wind was driven by the fury of Haroda, and seemed to be aimed directly at Nazir. The swirling wind lifted him up, and sucked him into a vortex of sand and stone. He tumbled over and over, like a discarded toy tossed carelessly by a child from a window. The sand was suffocating; the roar of the storm deafened him. Terrified, he thought he was going to die. Then, just as suddenly as the storm had started, it stopped. He fell from the grip of the vortex, and landed face down in the sand with a force that left him unconscious.

He had no idea how long he had been lying there, but slowly, he began to regain his senses. His eyes were stinging, and his ears were still drumming with the din of the storm, but now there was no sound; nothing stirred. He lay there for a long time without moving, his eyes tightly shut, listening. After a while, he began to feel the heat of the sand that covered him. He took a breath and then slowly opened his eyes, but could not see beyond the scarf that covered his eyes. Still, he did want to move, that is, until he heard the first call of the vultures overhead. Now, he had to move; otherwise, the predators circling above would begin their grim work.

Slowly, he raised himself to his hands and knees. He tossed his head back, and pushed the scarf from his eyes, but he was unprepared for what he saw. He shook his head, hoping to push the image out of his head. Perhaps, it was the storm that left him senseless. No, it was real. He shook his head again, this time in disbelief.

The sand of the desert had disappeared. The oasis that was in his sight just before the storm had also vanished. The sky was transformed; there was no sun. The air was so thick that it was difficult to take a breath. The coarse tan desert sand had somehow been transformed into a fine, red powder that became a choking dust when he took a handful. Above him, where there was once a deep blue sky, there was now a dull red cover – it was neither sky nor cloud. It seemed more like he was trapped under a suffocating veil. What was real was the overpowering smell in the air; it was the stench of death and decay.

He suddenly became aware that from the stillness, there was a faint sound. Had he imagined it? He held his breath, and closed his eyes to concentrate on the sound. Yes, there it was again. It sounded like someone whispering. To him, perhaps? But from where? Who?

"Ha!" the evil witch Haroda chortled. "You poor, ignorant fool. You have no idea where you are, do you? You are in the Zunir, the Land of Forgotten Souls. There is no salvation here, no hope for you and the other mortals who dared to defy me. You shall stay forever in this place of misery and despair. I can sense that you do not know who you really are and what your destiny is. Ha! Your destiny? Shall I tell you of your destiny? Your destiny is the Zunir!"

Nazir kept looking around in disbelief. How? Why? There were no answers, just confusion and a nagging fear. He continued to hear the raspy whisper in his head, but could not discern the words. He could not know that he was firmly in the grasp of the witch who would make his life a misery.

∞

Just as quickly as the vicious storm had lashed the hapless nomads, it ended. Arosh and the other elders in the tribe dug themselves out of the sand that had all but covered them. Everyone in the huddle had survived; the sheep were shaking off the sand. Despite its ferocity, Arosh gave thanks to the gods that no one had perished, but then there was the mystery of Nazir's fate. Lara, Nazir's mother, rushed over to the leader, "Arosh, Arosh, my Nazir, I cannot find him? Have you seen him? Where is he?" his mother asked in a terrified voice. Her face was searching Arosh for an answer. It told Arosh that this poor woman should not have to endure the loss of both her husband and now her son, but there would be no comfort.

"My dear, Lara, I don't know. I saw him leaving for the oasis to fetch water, but then the storm came up. Has he not returned?"

"Oh, no, then it is I who is to blame," she cried. "It was I who sent him." Lara turned her face away from Arosh, and looked into the vast empty desert. "Nazir, my beloved Nazir, where are you?"

Arosh put a hand on her shoulder and assured her that they would find Nazir. "Do not be alarmed, Lara. He probably sought shelter from the sandstorm and has yet to emerge from his hiding place. I will send several of the men to retrace his steps. We shall find him and return him to you." Privately, however, Arosh was not entirely convinced. There was something malevolent about this storm. This was more than a mere sandstorm; this was an act of pure evil.

CHAPTER 4

Gaius Fortus

Nazir had no idea how long he had been wandering in the Zunir. Hours, a day, a month? There was no way to tell. There was no way to determine direction – there were no stars at night, no sun during the day. The only light was the dull reddish haze that hung over the land. His every step kicked up clouds of choking red dust, and there was always the putrid smell of decay. He labored for every breath of air; it felt like he was breathing through a thin water reed.

He heard, or thought he heard, a whisper in the air. It was the sound of a woman calling to him. At first, he thought it was his mother, but it could not be. The desert was somehow too far away. No, this was someone else. Encouraging him not to despair? Now, it wasn't one voice; there were several. He was overhearing a conversation, and he thought it was about him. He closed his eyes to concentrate on the muted voices.

"No, Zoltan, I shall not release him. He is mine forever."

"You shall not have him, Haroda. You know who he is – the White Fire. Just as you cannot escape your fate, nor can he."

And so, the conversation went on. It was like a buzzing in his head. The two angry voices went back and forth. Were these the gods? But how could this be? And why were they debating about him? And why was he being called the "White Fire"? He felt as if he were being tried for an offense against the gods. As he looked around at his surroundings, he thought perhaps, he had already been tried and convicted, and was now being punished. He strained to listen. He could only discern snatches of sentences:

"Amira...trapped...hidden...Azurat...mine forever..."

"Release her...command you...beware...my wrath..."

He was so engrossed in the angry exchange that he did not notice the object in front of him. He tripped over it, and landed on top of the dark mass. It was a man. The figure rose up slowly and menacingly in front of Nazir like a ghost. He was at least two heads taller than Nazir but much, much older. Nazir had never seen anyone this old. The old man had long, matted white hair that hung down to his waist. His skin was pallid – almost gray, and his eyes were deep set and surrounded by dark circles. His clothes were in tatters. His long, gnarled fingers held a thick white staff that had the carved head of a snake on the knob end. In the eye sockets of the carving were two yellow jewels.

The old man was angry; his deep voice was cold and intimidating, "You clumsy fool. You nearly killed me." But it was the snakehead staff that frightened Nazir more. As the angry man spoke, the yellow snake eyes began to glow brighter and brighter until two flashes of light sprang from the eyes and surrounded Nazir. The lights formed a glowing white bubble around the young man. Nazir was terrified. He thought that a mysterious force had brought him here, and then there were the voices, and now this? Surely, this could only mean death is imminent.

"You? Can it be?" was all that the ghostly figure could manage. "It is **YOU**!" The old man staggered backward as if struck by a blow.

Nazir, still bathed in the harsh white light from the snake's eyes, backed away from the old man. Surely, this man is mad; he is here to kill me, thought Nazir.

"Can it be? Are you....? The man did not finish his sentence. He saw that the young man was terrified, and backing away from him as if to avoid a killing blow from the staff. His voice softened. "It's all right, it's all right," he tried to reassure Nazir. "I won't hurt you. I just can't believe it's you!" The bubble of the glowing light blinked out.

Nazir spoke first, from inside his glowing white bubble, "Are you here to kill me? Or am I already dead?"

"No, my boy, you are not dead; and I am most certainly not here to kill you. I did not recognize you at first. I am so sorry to have frightened you. I never thought that I would play a part in your destiny."

"Destiny?" replied Nazir, now more confused than terrified.

"Yes, your destiny," the man said slowly, "Your destiny, but it is clear to me that you do not know, do you?"

"Know, know what?" replied Nazir. "What destiny? Who are you? Where am I? Please, sir, I was lost in this place, and now I am confused because I don't know what you are talking about."

Fortus saw the confusion and fear in the young man's eyes. He thought the boy was telling the truth.

He had no idea of the forces that brought him to the Zunir and of the fate that awaited him. "Boy, I am Gaius Fortus, a broken old man, wizard, and prisoner of the evil Haroda." With a sweep of his hand, he said, "This, this is my prison, this forsaken place that they call the Zunir. I am here because I succumbed to the temptation of vanity. The witch, Haroda, told me that I would become the greatest of all sorcerers only on the condition that I pledge my total allegiance to her. I was a fool to believe her. See what my conceit and arrogance have brought me: a place in this hell for all eternity. Now, you know my name and why I am here. What is yours, young man?" Gaius Fortus asked in the hope of reassuring him.

"Nazir, sir, my name is Nazir. I live with my tribe in the Sagar desert. My leader is Arosh; my mother is Lara," the young man blurted out.

"Then, Nazir, son of Lara of the Sagar, come with me. You look like you have not eaten anything in days," the magician said. "Here, drink," the man said, offering a flask to the young man, who at first eagerly took it, but then, before he put the flask to his lips, he returned it to the magician and said, "Thank you, sir, but it is your water; you should drink first."

The two walked for some time. Gaius said nothing. For the old man, there was so much to do and so little time. Nazir was lost in all the questions he wanted to ask the old man, but thought the better of it, or at least until he had some food in his belly.

They walked in silence until they came upon a hollow in the side of a mountain that suddenly loomed up in a red mist. As they got closer to the hollow, Gaius quickened his pace. It was clear to Nazir that Gaius knew his way and was anxious to be in the safety of the mountain. As they got closer to the red wall, it appeared to Nazir, who was following closely behind, that Gaius was about to collide with the stone wall. To Nazir's surprise, Gaius pulled back a red curtain that served as a door and motioned for

Nazir to enter. For the first time, Nazir saw something that resembled the world from which he was torn by the sandstorm. How long ago was it now? How many days, or longer, had he been wandering in this mysterious land? He shook off the thought and looked around him. He saw a simple room with a bed, a table and a lamp. In the center of the room was a pool of water bubbling up from an underground spring. The warm glow of the lamp and the familiar features comforted him. Here was the first sign of normality in this bizarre world into which he had been thrust.

From within a cupboard under his bed, Gaius Fortus took some hard bread and dried meat and offered it to Nazir. For as hungry as he was, Nazir put up his hand and said, "Sir, I thank you for your generosity, but I cannot take what is rightly yours. I see that food is scarce in this forbidding world."

Gaius looked at the young man. *Yes,* he thought to himself, *this is the one – the White Fire.* Gaius was still holding the stick with the snake's head. He waved the stick; a blinding flash of light shot out from the snake's eyes, and in an instant, a feast appeared in front of the young man. Meats of all varieties, fruits, nuts and wine were arrayed on a low table.

"There," said the wizard, "Help yourself." For a moment, Nazir hesitated. He looked over to the old man and then back to the table. He gingerly reached out to touch a piece of fruit. Yes, he thought, it was real.

The man nodded to Nazir, "Go ahead. Eat. Eat all you want!"

CHAPTER 5

Nazir – The White Fire

Gaius listened intently to the young man who, in between large mouthfuls of food, recounted his life's history in the Sagar desert with his mother and the nomadic tribe, about the death of his father, and his life with his mother and their struggles to survive. He told the sorcerer about the uncertainty he faced as he approached manhood, particularly regarding the decision by the tribal elders whether to admit him to sit at the council fire. Nazir told the old man about the events that brought him to the Zunir – to this wasteland.

"Tell me about your mother, Lara," Gaius asked softly.

Nazir hesitated for a moment. He pictured her in his mind. What was she doing now? How was she coping alone? She must be so worried and sad. The old man saw the sadness that came over Nazir's face. "You must love your mother," Gaius offered.

"Yes. She's all I have, sir. She has cared for me and taught me so many things," replied Nazir. "I am worried what will become of her."

"Have no fear. She is well, and yes, you will see her again," said the sorcerer reading Nazir's thoughts.

Nazir was about to ask, "But, how did you know what I was thinking?" when Gaius interrupted him.

"Shall I tell you how you got here and why?" Gaius Fortus asked bluntly.

Nazir was stunned by the question. "Yes, sir, please do!" Nazir eagerly responded.

"First, I will tell you why you are here. That will help you understand how you find yourself in this forsaken world," he began. The wizard paused for a very long time. It seemed to Nazir as if he were looking deep into his soul. The silence was unbearable for the young man who looked at him intently, waiting for him to begin.

"You are the White Fire."

Nazir's head snapped back; his eyes widened like saucers. It hit him like thunder. He could not speak; his breath came in short bursts. The young man knew about the legends of the gods and their relationship with mortals, a relationship that was often turbulent and even violent. His father had told him of the legend of the White Fire – the one and only mortal ever endowed by the gods with great powers.

"I ...am the... White Fire?" Nazir said haltingly, "But how can this be? I am just a simple desert nomad. Look at me. Do I look like a warrior? I could not even pass the simple warrior's tasks from the Sagar Council of Elders. Who am I to earn such favor from the gods? Surely, you must be mistaken, sir."

Gaius Fortus looked at him with a mix of sadness and concern, "No, my son, you are the White Fire. It is your destiny. For a thousand years, no mortal has been deserving of such a gift from the greatest of the gods, Zoltan. There was one before you who lived during the Age of Beshat and then disappeared. Only Zoltan knows the reason. I have seen in a dream that you are to be the anointed one – the new White Fire. It is to you that we must all turn to restore justice and order, to be the model of virtue for mankind, and to save the world from the evil witch, Haroda, the Goddess of the Underworld, Galthoram. She has defied the gods, kidnapped Amira, the Earth Goddess, and stolen the Azurat – the life-giving force of the Earth. Her malevolence is like a disease that has spread from the Wadiri, the desert garden, to encompass all of the Earth. The Earth is now parched and withering; all living things are dying. Mankind has been corrupted. Everything has been thrown into darkness and peril. The White Fire is the only hope. And, it is you who must assume the mantle of the White Fire. It is you who must go forth and restore harmony in the universe. Even the gods look to you – they are powerless against Haroda. Only you, the White Fire, can win this battle."

Nazir listened with astonishment. "But if this is so, then why am I here in this forsaken place, Gaius? Surely, I cannot be the White Fire you speak of; I am just a prisoner here like you."

The old magician spoke slowly, "Once, many years ago, I was arrogant enough to believe that I, Gaius Fortus, would be the White Fire. I was a magician with considerable powers, more powerful than any other wizard in all the kingdoms. One day, I was visited by the evil witch, Haroda, the Goddess of the Underworld, Galthoram. I was bewitched by her stories of the White Fire. She said that I could be the White Fire, but first, I must pledge my life to her, for it was only through her that the White Fire derived his power over the Earth.

"So greatly was I enchanted by the thought of becoming the next White Fire that I agreed to her diabolical bargain. From that day forward, I became her slave; I did her bidding – whatever she asked. I committed atrocities against the innocent. When I asked her to fulfill her part of the bargain by anointing me as the White Fire, she laughed, 'You fool; you are nothing more than a circus performer. You could never be the White Fire. You are arrogant and egotistical. Only the pure of heart could ever be the White Fire and possess the power – there are no longer such mortals. You are all too weak.' And with that, she summoned a violent sandstorm which propelled me here in the Zunir – the land of the forgotten souls."

"But, sir, why am I here? What have I done to Haroda that she should cast me in this place, the Zunir?" asked Nazir plaintively. In his heart, however, he knew what Gaius Fortus would say.

"She saw in a dream that there was one such mortal who was pure of heart – blameless - and would be the White Fire – you, my son. You are to be the White Fire. Haroda could not risk having you free to fulfill your destiny. She knew that – unlike me – you would never succumb to the temptations of arrogance, vanity and selfishness. The only way she could keep you from becoming the White Fire was to cast you in the Zunir.”

“Then, like you, I am doomed to spend my days wandering here in this dreadful place? She has imprisoned me,” Nazir said glumly.

The magician smiled benignly. “No, my son, I am imprisoned here for my sins. You shall leave this place to take up the cause of the gods.”

Nazir frowned, raised his hand, and shook his head. “Stop, please! White Fire, Haroda, Amira, and my destiny. This is all too much. I don’t understand, sir. Why is this happening to me? I am not a warrior. Until now, my destiny was to wander the desert with my people – it is an uncomplicated way of life. We spend our days tending our herds and trading with other tribes. At night, we eat together, talk, sing and laugh. Now, you say I must 'take up the cause of the gods.' This is too much, sir. I... I cannot. Sir, I am a shepherd – not a warrior with a grand destiny. I talk to the stars at night and dream of flying into the heavens to touch them. I dream of floating in the sea with fish. Don't you see? There must be some mistake."

The old man listened to the young man as he struggled to make sense of all he had heard. There was a long silence. Nazir looked at Gaius plaintively.

"There is no mistake, Nazir. You are the White Fire," came the wizard's reply.

"If this is my destiny, Gaius, how will the gods transform this mere shepherd into a warrior?"

"I can teach you the skills of swordsmanship and combat, but you already possess the heart of a warrior, the heart of the White Fire. Are you ready?"

Nazir thought for a long time. He was to be the White Fire – it was just too difficult to comprehend. It was too large to take in. His head ached, and his arms and legs felt like dead weights. Nazir was feeling decidedly overwhelmed. This was all too much. At that moment, he just wanted to go home, have a meal with his mother, and sit under the stars.

"I cannot make such a decision in an instant," Nazir reminded Gaius. "I need some time; I need to speak to my mother and Arosh."

Gaius Fortus' reply was swift and pointed, "There is no time for lengthy reflection. You must decide here and now."

Gaius Fortus waited for the boy's reply. There was too little time to spend agonizing over his destiny. These were perilous times; action was required. Nazir thought, *if this is the will of the gods, who am I to challenge them? Was this not an honor to be the White Fire and to be chosen for such a world-changing mission? And yet, who am I to undertake such a dangerous mission? No, Gaius, I do not have the heart of a warrior; I am but a humble shepherd and happy to be so. The only sword I have ever held is the wooden sword my father made for me, and I failed in combat with the other boys of my tribe.*

Despite the internal struggle, and after what seemed an eternity, Nazir's face slowly changed. The pained expression was replaced by a look of resignation. The soon-to-be warrior closed his eyes, took a deep breath and nodded.

"Nazir?" Gaius interrupted his reverie.

His reply came in a whisper, "I...I am ready,"

"Well, then. Let's begin."

CHAPTER 6

The Mission

Gaius Fortus had been the greatest wizard of his day. He had used his magical powers to protect the weak and to right injustices, but because of his weakness – his vanity and arrogance – he had fallen from grace after succumbing to Haroda. However, despite his imprisonment in the Zunir, Zoltan, the greatest of the gods, had given him this opportunity to redeem himself for his past misdeeds. Now, he saw his purpose in life; he was the precursor of the White Fire. He, Gaius Fortus, would teach this young man the ways of a warrior-wizard, then set him on his path to become the White Fire, and save the Earth from the witch, Haroda, and rescue the Goddess Amira and recover the Azurat.

"Magic is like this pool," Gaius said, pointing to the pool of water in the center of the room. "It is deep, and at its deepest, it is dark, but at the surface, it draws the light from other sources. Put your hand in it, and it surrounds you; put your body in it, and it will carry you. You can drink it, and it will give you life. But like magic, the water can also be deadly. It can suffocate and drown you. So it is with magic. It is a potent force for both good and evil. In the hands of the just, like you, White Fire, magic can be used to ward off and destroy the forces of the evil Haroda."

Nazir noted that for the first time, Gaius did not use his given name. He addressed him as White Fire.

The old wizard was seated in a chair, holding the staff. He leaned forward and thrust the staff forward. Nazir noted that the knurled stick with the snake carving on the knob end was a simple branch cut from the eucalyptus tree. "See, White Fire, to most, this staff is nothing more than a walking stick, but in the hands of the purest of the pure - your hands - this staff has unimaginable power. I can only perform simple magic tricks, but you shall be able to summon the power of the gods." At that moment, the yellow snake eyes glowed brightly. They seemed to come alive and fix their cold eyes on him. Nazir shivered.

"Do not be afraid. Take it. I no longer have need of it. You are its master now; it will answer now only to you," the magician said. His face was flushed with excitement.

Nazir reached out and took it.

At that moment, an explosion of white light filled the room. It blinded both Nazir and the old magician. Nazir and Gaius were thrown face down; neither dared to look up. Out of the blinding flash came a voice that rolled like thunder.

"I am Zoltan, the greatest of the gods. Nazir, henceforth, you shall be the White Fire. You shall be my sword, and I shall be your shield.

You shall be the banner of virtue, honor and justice for all the people of the world. Serve me well. The Earth and all creation flow through my beloved Amira. Without her, the land is parched; nothing will grow; and the people are like wheat, corn and barley, they will wither and die. Find the lost Goddess Amira, recover the Azurat, and restore the Earth to its fullness. Send the witch to the depth of Galthoram. Protect the mortals and serve them. This is your duty; this is your destiny."

As quickly as it came, the light went out, and there was silence. Nazir's hand felt as if it had been welded to the stick. Gaius looked up at Nazir. The young man's face had somehow been transformed. He had lost the boyish look. His eyes were piercing; his face had a determined look. He had the air of a man, self-assured and ready. As Nazir, the White Fire, stood, it seemed to Gaius that the White Fire had even grown in stature. Nazir looked down at the old man and offered his hand to help him. The young man's hands were now strong and hard but gentle to the touch. Gaius started to kneel before this man – the White Fire - but Nazir stopped him. In a gentle but firm voice, Nazir said, "Gaius, my friend, my teacher, I am now ready. Let us begin." Yes, Gaius thought, the transformation had indeed just taken place. Now, the White Fire was truly ready to fulfill his destiny.

∞

Lara had not slept peacefully for weeks. She listened for every sound, hoping that the next one would be her Nazir entering the tent with the water bucket in hand. She waited for him to say, "I am here, mother. I'm hungry." But it was not to be. She felt that she had delivered her only son to his death in the storm.

One night during fitful sleep, it came to her in a dream. She was standing in the middle of an open field when a white cloud descended from the heavens and enveloped her. She heard a voice like the rumble of thunder from an oncoming storm, but it was not threatening,

"Lara, your son, Nazir, lives. He is fulfilling his destiny at my command. He is the White Fire."

Before the cloud lifted, she had the briefest glimpse of her son. He was bathed in a brilliant white light. To his mother, Nazir had changed. He stood erect and determined. In his hand, he was carrying a large stick. Then, for an instant, she saw her son as she remembered him: his face was gentle and he was smiling...and then he was gone.

"Wait, my son. Where are you? Will you ever return?" But there was no answer. Although confused by the dream, she was comforted by the thought that her son was alive. She had heard of the legend of the White Fire, but could not imagine that her son, her gentle boy, would become the White Fire under the command of the gods.

CHAPTER 7

"Al haber, al asham"

For days, Gaius spoke to the White Fire about the power of magic, the incantations, the spells, and the secret words that could conjure up forces of good and evil. He spoke to him about the power of the worn staff with the snake's head that now never left Nazir's hands. "As a magician, I could only make simple magic tricks with that staff, but for you, White Fire, the power of the staff is beyond magic; the power comes from within you now. You and the staff are one and the same. You only need to utter the words *"Al haber, al asham"* (translated: "I command you to serve"), and it will respond to your every command. With this staff, you can summon the forces of the universe, the spirit world, and the power of the gods themselves. This staff is your sword and your shield. In your hands, White Fire, you and the staff can bring the witch, Haroda, to her knees, save Amira and return the Azurat, and, in so doing, save all mankind."

Nazir quickly learned from his master that his newly discovered determination to fulfill his role as the White Fire was merely the first step on a very long path. He must learn to understand and control this power – not necessarily an easy task. And, it was not to be used frivolously. Nazir's first utterance of "Al haber, al asham," produced a large flock of sheep in the cave that became frightened by the fire, causing a stampede in the magician's little room. The second was equally disastrous: "Al haber, al asham, give us fire, a roast and water," produced an avalanche of water that nearly drowned the pair. Other incantations produced a tornado in the room that destroyed all the furniture. In one near-catastrophic attempt to perfect his aim, Nazir pointed the staff at the magician, and let loose a tongue of flame that left the magician's hair singed and smoldering.

Gaius Fortus bore all these attempts with calmness, patience and mostly, good humor. "No, no, White Fire, you must not merely utter the words. The command must come from within your heart. At the moment you utter the words, you become a channel to the gods. You and the staff are merely instruments. Try again."

Over and over, the young man practiced with the staff. Some of the attempts produced peals of laughter from both the magician and his young pupil. Nazir tried turning the staff into an enormous broad sword, but it was so heavy that it caused its young warrior to fall forward, driving the point of the sword into the wall, leaving the old man holding his side with pains from laughter. Nazir's preoccupation with using the staff to produce food and water generally ended either in being flooded with water or, in one instance, nearly being crushed by tons of cabbage falling from the ceiling.

"Master, I cannot do it," the frustrated Nazir exclaimed. "This staff shall be the death of me."

"Yes, you can," Gaius replied, trying unsuccessfully to stifle his laughter. The old magician thought to himself that this was going to take longer than he expected, but he knew that, ready or not, the young man would need to confront his future sooner rather than later. The gods would most assuredly protect the boy from his enemies, but judging by the way Nazir handled the staff, he would also need protection from himself.

"Come, White Fire, let us rest before you and the staff cause any more damage. My humble home looks more like a war zone, and the stench of rotting cabbage is overwhelming."

Nazir turned the head of the staff around and looked into its glowing yellow eyes. "See what you have done! You must obey my every command."

Whereupon, another storm of water and cabbage fell, this time only on him. Turning to Gaius, he said, "I wonder who is the master of whom."

Gaius surveyed the scene and just shook his head. This was indeed going to be a challenge. Putting his hand to his forehead, he said, "Perhaps, you can beg the staff to clean and repair my home."

CHAPTER 8

Cave of Sorrows

She awoke screaming, hurling curses at the gods, especially at Zoltan. She had heard Zoltan anointing Nazir as the White Fire. To Haroda, those words felt like a hot poker on her skin.

"He will not succeed; I shall defeat him, all of them. The Azurat is mine!" she shrieked.

Despite her defiance, Haroda felt a shiver of fear. She was facing the mighty Zoltan, the gods and now the White Fire. For all her awesome powers as the queen of Galthoram, she knew that the White Fire possessed forces that could be her downfall. Unlike the simple deception that proved to be the undoing of Gaius Fortus, she knew that a true White Fire could not be swayed by flattery, vanity and deceit. He was the true White Fire, pure of heart, blameless and committed to justice and equality for all people, and a servant of Zoltan in the quest to save mankind from evil – Haroda. She immediately summoned all the dark forces of Galthoram, and ordered them to surround her to protect her from the White Fire.

∞

The training was intense and without pause. Nazir was a quick study with the staff, and finally learned the incantations necessary to release the forces in his command. With every passing week, his confidence as the White Fire grew. As Gaius watched the White Fire practice with the staff, he asked himself whether Nazir was ready for the enormous task ahead of him. Did he truly understand his mission and the many obstacles he faced that would challenge not only his endurance but also his determination? Gaius knew that time was growing short. "White Fire, we must leave here immediately."

"But, master, I have only begun my training; I need more time to perfect these techniques."

Gaius replied, "I understand, White Fire, but time is not in our favor. Surely, by now, the witch Haroda knows that you have been anointed and that you are ready to confront her. She has most certainly prepared herself together with the dark forces at her disposal and will come to kill you. She will not rest and will attack you relentlessly until she destroys the White Fire. I know of a way to leave here. It is the through the Cave of Sorrows. Come, we must go, now."

They walked together for hours through the bleak, red-baked Zunir. Not a word was spoken; each was absorbed in his own thoughts. Nazir broke the silence when the entrance to the cave loomed out of the red haze, "Gaius, the cave: let us make haste."

Gaius stopped at the entrance and turned to Nazir, "I am not going with you. I cannot, White Fire. Only the blameless may pass through. Anyone who attempts to enter the cave who is not pure of heart will face unspeakable agony and be tortured by their guilt."

"But, how am I to pass through this cave?"

Gaius reassured the young warrior, "You are the White Fire, the purest of the pure. You don't need a map or even a guide. You will know where you are. The staff will be your compass." The old man hesitated for a moment, put his arm on Nazir's shoulder, and then spoke as a father would, "Go, my son, do not be afraid. Your cause is just. You will find a way to defeat her."

"But what about you? What will become of you?" Nazir asked, touched by the man's gentle manner.

"I will be all right, White Fire. Defeat Haroda and then, and only then, will I be freed from this. Now go."

Nazir turned and walked into the cave. He turned around for a final glance at his mentor, but Gaius was gone.

He looked around him to get his bearings. The ceiling of the cave seemed to disappear into the blackness, as did the walls and his path ahead. He observed that it was less a cave but more a black box. He quickly lost all sense of direction. Even the entrance had disappeared. At that moment, he began to hear a moaning he had never heard before. It was not from pain but more from a profound and abiding sadness. The moan was joined by others – more and more, until this chorus of despair was so overpowering that Nazir called out, "Who are you? Why do you carry on so?"

A disembodied voice spoke, "We are the lost, confronted by our past misdeeds, and condemned to relive the pain and agony caused by them. If you have brought pain or sorrow to another by your transgressions, then you too shall wither and die here with us."

"I have not sinned, nor harmed or brought sorrow to any other."

"If you have sinned, she will find you; if you have sinned, she will find you; if you have sinned, she will find you," came the mournful repeated refrain in reply.

Nazir raised the staff with its yellow eyes blazing. "Then, begone. You cannot help me. I shall find her and bring all of this to an end."

The voices suddenly stopped, and Nazir was left alone in the pitch black of the Cave of Sorrows. He lifted the staff into the darkness and uttered the words, "Al haber, al asham, give me light." With that, the snake's head at the end of the staff erupted into a blinding white light. The blazing shaft of light seemed to come from the snake's eyes, but the staff itself was not burning. The light penetrated deep into the cave, revealing a stone pathway that twisted ahead into the darkness. With the staff as a torch, Nazir stepped forward. He had not taken more than a dozen steps when suddenly a large, hideous face appeared in the light. It was twisted in agony; tears of blood flowed from the eyes, and a greenish sludge oozed from the ears and nose.

The terrifying face advanced slowly, menacingly. As it loomed closer to Nazir, he was nearly overcome with the stench.

The repulsive face spoke. "You are Nazir, the desert nomad who has been summoned by Zoltan on a quest to defeat Haroda. I am Lashot, the embodiment of the evil that you mortals perpetrate. Surely, you are not without blame. No mortal can be without sin. Only the blameless may pass here. If you are not the purest of the pure, I, Lashot, will devour your flesh, spit you up, and devour you again. I shall repeat this every day for eternity. Beware, Nazir, take one more step forward, and you shall be mine."

"I have not sinned against any man. I am without blame, guilt or sin. I am the White Fire. My soul is as pure as this white light. Let me pass!" demanded Nazir.

Hearing the words "White Fire," the beastly visage began to choke. Its eyes bulged out of its head. "How can this be? A White Fire – the purest of the pure? Impossible! Blasphemy!" the beast shouted in between coughing. "Pass this test, and I shall let you pass to the other side. Fail and I will consume you with particular pleasure for your blasphemy." With that, the ogre conjured up a windstorm that encircled Nazir. It whirled and screamed around him. The wind nearly blinded him and tore at his already tattered clothes. It coiled around his limbs with a force that sucked the air from his lungs. "Confess your sins, mortal! You have wronged others, have you not? Confess and be judged!" the creature screamed at Nazir. Round and round, the wind twisted and turned like a snake about to devour its prey.

But Nazir held fast. "Never! I am the White Fire – the purest of the pure. I have wronged no man. I am without sin in my heart. Begone beast. Return to the pit of doom. You shall not have me!"

Suddenly, the violent wind stopped. The massive, grotesque face screeched, and just as suddenly as it appeared, it vanished. There was total silence. Now, in front of him, Nazir, the White Fire, saw a distant light – daylight. As he approached the end of the Cave of Sorrows, he could still hear the mournful cries of the doomed souls.

He stepped out into the hot and dry desert sun and smelled the sweet desert air – home. It felt good to be away from the red dust of the Zunir and the Cave of Sorrows. He closed his eyes for a moment, took a very deep breath, and stepped forward. It had become clear what he must do, and nothing and no one would stand between him and the fulfillment of his mission, his destiny.

CHAPTER 9

The Craxon & The Volarian Warlocks

Lashot, the tormentor of souls in the Cave of Sorrows, emerged from the dark shadows and knelt before Haroda. The ghostly apparition's raspy voice filled the dimly lit chamber, "Queen of Darkness, Mistress of Galthoram, I have seen the one they call the White Fire. He has emerged from the Cave of Sorrows and now seeks you."

Haroda jumped from her throne as if catapulted into the air. She screamed, "How can this be? No one but the purest of the pure could ever survive the torment of the Lashot. There is no such mortal, not even this White Fire!"

She paced furiously in the chamber, repeating over and over, "How can this be? There is no such mortal! This White Fire must be stopped," she screamed to all the dark spirits of Galthoram. "His powers are that of a mere mortal. What can these so-called powers be in the face of mine? I shall bring the demons and the fiends of hell to crush him! Nothing and no one shall take what is mine. Both the Earth and what lies beneath are my domain – forever. Amira is my slave, and the Azurat is the jewel that I now wear around my neck as the symbol of my majesty and power over the Earth."

She turned to the dark phantom. "Where is he now?" she demanded from Lashot.

"He roams the desert in search of you," came the hoarse reply. He nears the village of Jabhar."

Haroda raised her arms and called out for the Craxon, a dark spirit who inhabited the desert and manifested itself in the form of an enormous dragon composed of desert sand. "Craxon, Sand Dragon, I command you. Arise." Suddenly, the ground began to shake violently, sand started to swirl and twist, the wind screamed, and the sky darkened. The monster formed and re-formed as the wind churned the sand. Out of the whirling mass of sand, the Craxon, the Sand Dragon, finally took shape and slowly arose – a massive, misshapen beast that was terrifying to look at. Its eyes were black and fierce; its fangs were like a thousand shards of glass; and it had claws as long as spears that glowed white hot. The Craxon's roar was deafening and so fierce that Haroda stepped back lest she be consumed by its fiery breath. "Who commands the Craxon?" it bellowed.

"It is I, Haroda, Queen of the Dark, who commands you to obey," the witch called.

"What is it you wish of me?" came the snarling reply.

"Find the one they call the White Fire. It was you who brought him to me in the Zunir, but he has escaped. Find him now, and destroy him!"

"It shall be done," the Sand Dragon roared in reply. With that, the Craxon thundered off into the distance in search of his prey.

Nazir had been walking day and night for three days under the blistering desert sun and through the bone-chilling night. He would not stop until he had accomplished his mission. Amira was Haroda's hostage, and the Azurat stone was now hanging around the witch's neck. There was no time to waste. The Earth was dying with each day that he, the White Fire, delayed. He must find the evil enchantress and end her reign of terror. His thoughts were abruptly cut short when he heard a familiar sound – the growing roar of a sandstorm approaching him, just as the storm that threw him into the Zunir. He turned to see the Craxon looming larger and larger as it roared down on him. This time, however, Nazir was prepared. No longer was he the helpless desert boy from a tribe of nomads. He was the White Fire.

The Craxon was nearly upon him. The sand dragon's eyes flashed with anger, and his fangs were bloodied with the ill-fated victims who had fallen in his path. The dragon's tail violently slashed back and forth, creating a dust storm that blotted out the sky. When the monster spoke, the roar sounded like thunder; it shook the ground underneath Nazir. "You, mortal, you shall die. Your destiny is to die before me like the insect that you are." The Craxon reared back, and unleashed a torrent of fire at the young warrior.

Nazir raised his staff. The snake eyes glowed a golden yellow. "Al haber, al asham. Give me a shield." At that very instant, a flash of white light encompassed Nazir. The sheer force of the sandstorm forced him to his knees. He could feel the heat from the Craxon's tongue of flame, but the force glanced harmlessly off his shield.

Nazir raised his staff. The snake eyes began to glow brighter still. "Al haber, al asham. Give me thunder, lightning and torrents of rain."

In an instant, the clear blue sky turned dark as night as black clouds covered the sun. The thunder was so loud that it drowned out the roar of the Craxon. The lightning struck the hellish creature repeatedly. And then, suddenly, the roiling clouds let loose a torrent of water that fell on top of the Craxon. The sand dragon let out a scream that nearly deafened the White Fire, but the pillar of water kept falling on the Craxon, who writhed in agony until the creature had been reduced to a pile of mud. The screaming stopped, and the clouds gave way to the sun.

Nazir glanced at the patch of now wet sand, and said aloud, so she could hear: "Haroda, you cannot stop me from my destiny. I shall rescue the Goddess Amira and reclaim the Azurat for her. I am coming for you. Save yourself. Surrender them to me, and I will spare you. If not, I shall see that you perish in the depths of Galthoram."

Haroda heard the desert boy – now the White Fire. A shiver of fear passed over her. So, it must be true. This boy, this mere mortal, was indeed the legendary White Fire that Zoltan had anointed, protected, and who now had the power to escape death. He had escaped the Zunir, passed through the Cave of Sorrows, and now defeated the Craxon. Her rage mixed with growing fear. The witch flew into a frenzy, flying in dizzying circles in her chamber, smashing whatever was within her reach. She screamed from her dark cavern, "Never! White Fire you may be, but you shall never defeat me. Never!"

Suddenly, she stopped in mid-air; a deadly silence filled the chamber. She tapped her gnarled fingers on her lips and began to ponder on how she could outwit this cursed boy and his protector, Zoltan. She must devise a plan, a plan that would crush both White Fire and Zoltan. "I must find a way to stop this invader in my domain. He is, after all, a mere mortal, and mortals can die. Yes, White Fire, perhaps, it was your good fortune and the intervention of Zoltan that you have managed to escape me. You may be undefeated thus far, but your luck cannot last forever, and your protectors, the gods, will not always be so watchful. I will find a way; I will devise a plan. You will not elude me again."

She knew she must strike again, and soon in order to stop the advancing desert warrior. Zoltan would probably be celebrating the boy's victory over the Craxon. So, the gods would never expect a second strike. Yes, she would strike again. This time she would not risk sending one lone spirit to engage this White Fire. Her cunning plan was really quite simple. She would send the entire troop of Guardians of the Galthoram, the dreaded Volarian Warlocks. These were the most feared of the hellish creatures that inhabited the dark reaches of the underworld. The Volarian were faceless in their hooded black robes that flared around them as they floated above the chamber. They were neither body nor spirit – more like an evil apparitions. They could wield an axe like any warrior, but they could also invade an opponent's body like an infection and possess that person's soul.

They were the conjurers of suffering for each of the souls condemned to Galthoram. They crafted unimaginable pain and torture for their victims. They could create personal demons that possessed the condemned for eternity. These were Haroda's sorcerers and masters of black magic. Together, they would conjure up a bestial image that was itself the sum of Nazir's worst fears and nightmares. The Volarian Warlocks could penetrate the White Fire's defenses not only with sword and fire, but also with visions and dreams – terrifying visions and nightmares that would overwhelm the desert boy and invade his soul.

The witch raised both arms and screamed, "Warlocks! Warlocks! I command you to come before me. Now! Warlocks!"

The Warlocks emerged or rather materialized silently from somewhere in the darkness, from the very bowels of the Galthoram. The air suddenly died, replaced with the stench of decay. There was deadly silence. Their robes were black, flowing, and hooded. The Warlocks filled the chamber in every direction as far as the eye could see. There were so many of the creatures that it was impossible to distinguish one from another. They appeared as one dark, ominous mass. They remained floating in the massive chamber, waiting.

"You, my elite warriors, you must defeat this one who is called the White Fire. He brings a calamity upon us all. He is Zoltan's spear to strike at us; he would deny us our rightful place in the universe. Destroy him, and I shall reward you. You shall have him for yourselves to punish for his insolence. Fail, and the same fate shall befall you as the Craxon. You will wander the middle world – neither in the heavens with the gods, nor with me in Galthoram –

yours will be an eternity of self-torment. Now, go. Find the White Fire, and kill him."

Nazir pushed himself forward. He was exhausted, but he would allow himself neither food nor rest. Time was running out for the Earth. If he did not save Amira and the Azurat, the Earth would surely continue to wither, and then die. All about him, he saw the encroaching death of the Earth. The oases he passed on his journey were dying slowly: there was barely any water; the tall palms had yellowed; the grass had been seared as if by a flame. He allowed himself to think of his mother, Lara, and Arosh, the leader of the tribe. How far away they seemed. How long had it been since he saw them? It seemed so long ago. Life was so simple then, but now he was the White Fire on a mission to save the Earth. He needed to rescue Amira and the Azurat before it was too late.

He had hardly finished the thought when again he found himself thrown face forward into the burning sand. It stung his eyes and burned his cheeks. He could hardly breathe, such was the force pressing down on him. But then he felt something worse, something he had never felt in his entire young life. Despite the desert heat, he felt as if his blood had turned to ice water.

The Volarian Warlocks had found him. They immediately surrounded the young warrior, but remained suspended just a few feet over his head. There were so many that they blocked the sun, so much so that it became as dark as midnight. There was no sound; nothing stirred. The air around him seemed to vanish. The young warrior nearly gagged with the rotten smell of the Warlocks. His breath came in short bursts as the crushing weight of the Warlocks continued to press on his chest.

From inside the black mass came a harsh, raspy whisper, "Nazir, Nazir, look, look into your heart."

Despite all his newly acquired power, White Fire felt a terror overcome him. "See, it is your father," a chorus of hollow voices chanted in unison. Nazir was young when his father died of a fever. Often at night, when he was alone with the stars, Nazir would try hard to remember his father's face. It would come to him like a mist in the sky, and then, like a cloud, dissolve and evaporate. As he lay there, pressed face forward in the scorching sand, struggling to breathe, he saw a face and heard a voice, and as he did so, the White Fire began to enter a dream world unlike one he had ever seen. He began to float in this ethereal space. There was neither an up or down – just an eerie feeling of weightlessness. Then he heard an unworldly whisper, but it was a familiar voice, one he had heard many times long ago.

"Nazir, Nazir, my son."

The weight on Nazir suddenly lifted. He stood up and began to follow the soothing, faraway voice. A ghostly face appeared and beckoned to him with a slow wave of its hand, "Come, my son. It is I, your father." The White Fire found himself in an oasis where the sky was painted with vivid oranges, reds, and blues mixing in long streaks – like the sky of a desert sunset, but there was no sun that he could see. The air was still, and a thick mist surrounded him, making each breath a deliberate one. Nazir saw a deep pool of crystal-clear water. He had never seen such clarity in an oasis. On one side of the pool, there was a carpet of pale green ferns. On the opposite edge, there was a sheer wall of dark, forbidding stone that seemed to emerge from the depths of the pool. He could see that the pool was deep, but such was its clarity that he saw or thought he saw the bottom as if it were a fingertip away.

"Nazir, I am your father, come to me." The voice was soothing.

Yes, he thought, this weathered face is my father. The face was now in front of Nazir, floating several feet in the air. The apparition glided in the direction of the pool of water. Nazir followed as if in a trance. His father's face was strong but kindly, and his eyes were gentle and inviting. His father's skin showed the ravages of the sun over the years, but still, the man was handsome despite his age. Nazir's eyes now opened, and closed in slow motion. His thoughts were coming slowly and unclearly. Through his haze, he saw his father suspended above the pool. Nazir edged closer to the pool. His father was smiling. Yes, he remembered now.

"Father, father, I have missed you so," Nazir said softly.

The White Fire reached out to the outstretched hand that was offered to him by his father. Nazir took several steps. The water in the pool was warm and inviting as he waded in up to his waist. As he did so, he felt as if he were being wrapped in a blanket, just as he was when he was a child complaining of the cold desert night.

Nazir was a little boy again. He spoke to his father. "Father, where have you been? May we play swords again?"

He went further into the pond as he walked with his father and then slipped silently under the water.

The blanket covered him. He was so tired, and now it was so peaceful. If he could just close his eyes for a few moments and feel the love and warmth of his father's arms around him.

He was about to close his eyes and release his staff when he felt the searing pain from a Volarian blade that pierced his chest. The fatherly figure suddenly turned into a skeleton. From its eye sockets, black worms poured out, and shredded cloth hung on its arms and legs. Where there was once his father's warm bosom, there was now only a hollow cavity filled with venomous snakes. At the same time, he heard the howls from the Warlocks as they celebrated their victory.

"We have killed the White Fire!" they screeched in unison, over and over. "We have killed the White Fire!"

Nazir struggled to breathe as blood poured from his chest. At first, he was overcome with a mix of loathing, anger and fear, but then he found himself again in a dreamlike state – not from the spell cast by the Warlocks, but by the loss of blood. He was sinking further into the deep water. The pain was falling away – there was growing darkness. A wave of peaceful feelings began to overtake him. So, he thought, this is what it is like to die. As he sank deeper into the pool, he could vaguely see the faceless black creatures floating around him, continuing their dark chorus, "We have killed the White Fire!"

He sank further into the depths of the pool. Just as he was slipping into unconsciousness, he dimly realized that his hand still had a tight grip on his staff. He half thought and half whispered, "Al haber, al asham. Please help me." Suddenly, the staff came to life. This otherwise simple branch of the eucalyptus tree grew larger and larger in the White Fire's hand. The eyes of the snakehead carving on the end of the stick flashed bolts of light as bright as the sun. The stick grew larger still. The wood was no longer thick and gnarled, but had now turned scaly and flexible.

It grew larger and larger...

The staff was now the width of a tree trunk and as tall as a palm tree. The snake's head turned from a decoration at the end of the staff into the head of a fierce and violent dragon. Nazir could no longer feel his hands around the staff but could feel himself being held by what seemed, in his dim conscious mind, a large hand. No, it was a large claw.

Larger still...

The claw curled around him so that he was now inside a massive fist. When it seemed that he could no longer breathe, he felt the water drain away from the claw. The dragon was now so large that it had outgrown the breadth and depth of the pool. With a roar that shook the Earth, the giant beast flew into the air. The entire Volarian army of Warlocks attacked the monster. They cast spells, conjured other beasts, and shot thousands of poisoned arrows – all to no avail. The monster grew larger until it had grown as high as the clouds floating over the desert. The creature's menacing yellow eyes narrowed as it prepared to strike. The hideous dragon-snake reared back, and from its enormous fanged mouth, it spit a fire that was as hot as the sun – white hot – at the Warlocks. The Warlocks were helpless in the face of such a flame that consumed them, and in a flash, they disintegrated into ashes.

The dragon roared, witch, you shall not have him, try as you might. He is my White Fire. It is his destiny."

The dragon opened its mighty claw in which Nazir lay unconscious. In the beast's palm, Nazir looked no larger than an ant. Then the giant creature blew a gentle wind from its nostrils onto Nazir. **"Awaken, Nazir, White Fire. Fulfill your destiny."**

With that, there was a blinding flash of light. Nazir found himself, once again, face forward in the hot sand. He slowly got to his knees and looked around. The only evidence of the Volarian army were piles of gray ash now blowing away in the desert wind. The wound in his chest was gone. Still in his grip was the staff – the yellow eyes of the snake were still glowing. In that instant, it became so clear; he understood completely. Through the staff, he was wholly connected to Zoltan, Lord of Lords and Master of the Universe. His existence, his very soul, was an extension of Zoltan.

Nazir stood up. "Yes, my lord, Zoltan. I am the White Fire. I shall fulfill my destiny."

Nazir raised the snakehead staff and looked up into the blue desert sky and called out, "Al aber, al asham. Tell me where I must go." The snakehead's yellow eyes glowed brightly once again. Nazir caught his breath as he felt the instruction enter his mind as if it were spoken aloud. The message was clear: go to the village of Jabhar that lay directly ahead. With that, Nazir set off.

CHAPTER 10

Village of Jabhar

Nazir had followed the old trade routes for three more days to reach the village of Jabhar, the home of the Karash people. They, too, were once nomads, fiercely independent people, who had decided to settle in the middle of the vast desert plain to protect that freedom, to escape their enemies and to find peace. Few, if any, would dare to cross the blistering desert to attack the Karash. Instead of living by spears and swords, the Karash had built a thriving village around a large oasis to provide comfort to other wandering tribes, and to sell food grown on farms irrigated by the cool waters fed by deep underground springs. However, Haroda's wickedness had spread throughout the world, leaving this once lush village barren and dying.

As he reached the crest of a dune, Nazir peered through the waving heat lines streaming up from the desert sand to see the village of Jabhar in the distance. The sun, now at its high point in a cloudless sky, beat down on him mercilessly as he trudged through the sand. He was thoroughly exhausted after his encounters with the Craxon and with the Valerian Warlocks. His throat was parched and his lips were cracked. His legs were burning with fatigue; several times, he stumbled to his knees. He was so tired that he needed the aid of the snakehead staff to raise himself. He longed for a bed other than sand and some food, but nothing could keep him from his mission. With every step and stumble, he became all the more determined. More than anything, he wanted to be in the company of friendly people – anything would be better right now than the endless desert, beasts and hordes of evil spirits intent on killing him. As he reached the tattered walls of Jabhar, the greeting was anything but friendly.

The sentries saw him approaching in the distance in a white cloak with a hood that covered his face. The hooded man was carrying a staff. He stumbled from time to time in the sand. They could see he was alone and, as such, posed little threat, unless, of course... unless, of course, the figure was Haroda herself in disguise, or one of her evil emissaries who had come to kill the remaining souls in the village. Within minutes of the alarm, the few able-bodied people in the village had gathered at the gate, armed with bows and arrows and spears. If this were to be their last stand, they would make Haroda earn her victory at a high price. There was to be no retreat, no hiding behind barricades. It would be a pitched battle to the end.

Nazir was lost in his thoughts when he suddenly heard the whine of an arrow flying through the air. He looked up to see it fall inches in front of him. The snake's yellow eyes at the head of his staff instantly began to glow brighter. "No, my guardian, we must not strike them," he whispered to the end of the walking stick. "They are frightened. Look at what Haroda has done to them," he continued as he looked at the decimated village. He stopped, pulled down the hood shielding his face, and instantly felt the blast of the sun's heat. He raised both his arms in the air and called out, "My friends, I am Nazir from the Shalari tribe over the mountains where the sun sets. I mean you no harm. I only ask for the welcome that is the custom of the desert people."

The leader of the guards called back, "Nazir, you may be, but how do we know that this is not a trick by the evil witch who wishes to see us all dead."

"I mean you no harm," Nazir said again. "I only ask for a drop of water, some food and a place to rest. I shall be on my way with the rising sun. You may stand guard over me throughout the night if it pleases you."

"Come forward slowly," replied the guard. "Keep your arms above your head." The archers drew back their bows, and the lancers held their spears at the ready as the young man approached them.

Nazir, sensing that his protective staff was becoming agitated at the threatening array of arms, again whispered to the knob now high in the air. "Be calm, my friend, be calm. I can sense that they are more frightened than threatening." Just in case he might be wrong, he whispered again to the serpent at the end of the staff, "But please be vigilant." The snake's eyes seemed to glow in understanding.

Surrounded now by swords and daggers, Nazir was led through the gates into the village. As he was marched to the great hall, he saw only desolation, despair and death around him. Many of the buildings lay in ruins as if hit by a fiery blast. The gushing spring was now barely a trickle. The village walls were crumbling, and the proud and gaudy turrets sitting atop the homes of wealthy merchants had fallen from their perches. The streets, once filled with stalls teaming with dates, figs, oranges and lemons, and shopkeepers hawking their merchandise, were now empty and silent. Jabhar had become a village of ghosts – no more than an arid and dusty stopover by other nomadic tribes crossing the desert. Many of the villagers had abandoned their homes; some had died of hunger and thirst. The desperate remainder was now huddled together in the decaying great hall of the village. Those brave enough to venture into the street seemed to be in a trance. They moved slowly, almost painfully, never lifting their downcast heads. Nazir was escorted through the vacant streets and alleys to their great hall. The entrance to the hall showed all the marks of bygone glory. The doors were imposing structures at least five meters in height and made of rare wood. The hinges and trim were gilded with gold, but now faded by sun and neglect. At the entrance to the great hall, he stopped momentarily. The chamber was dark. He blinked several times, trying to adjust his eyes to the dim light. A shove from the handle of a sword into his back pushed him into the room. He felt the cool air, and it made his skin tingle. He took a deep breath; it felt good to be out of the heat, although he was not certain about the reception from his hosts.

He observed that the chamber itself was lit only by slits in the wall at the top of the room itself. There was no fire, no music, no laughter – only the stony silence, and the stares of the wary Karashi elders.

As he stepped forward, he could see they were watching his every move. They were suspicious of this young man carrying the snakehead staff. Rumors had reached them about a young warrior anointed as the White Fire whose mission was to defeat the evil witch, Haroda. However, this was a mere boy before them. How could that be? It was either a trick by the witch herself, or the gods had taken leave of their senses by anointing so young a boy to assume such a momentous task: the salvation of mankind.

From the center of the assembled group, a tall man stepped forward. Despite the travails that had beset the village of Jabhar and his advancing years, the man stood proud and erect. His hair had remained black as cinders; his jaw jutted out; his eyes were a deep aquamarine. He wore the simple black robes of a desert nomad with a gold dagger in his belt. It struck Nazir that this was no ordinary man. What impressed the young man most were the elder's eyes. They were penetrating and probing. The tribal leader looked directly at Nazir without saying a word. It felt as if the man's eyes were peering into Nazir's soul. The leader did not take his eyes off the young warrior. Long moments of silence passed. It felt to Nazir like forever. He only heard the occasional cough.

The man stepped forward, taking his eyes off Nazir only for a moment to glance at the snakehead on the end of the staff. The man noted the soft glow of the yellow eyes. The silence was finally broken. "I am Sha Ram. You are welcome in our humble village, my young friend. Forgive the discourteous introduction, but these are perilous times. Please accept our hospitality." Nazir exhaled, relieved. Whatever the test, whatever the man saw, he had been satisfied.

"What is your name, young man?" Sha Ram enquired.

"Nazir," came the simple reply.

The leader turned to the others in the room. "Nazir of the Shalaris shall be our guest," he stated authoritatively, leaving no room for discussion. "Please, provide our guest with fresh clothes and a bath." He turned to Nazir and said, "We shall dine when you are ready."

"Thank you, sir. I am in your debt."

"You shall tell us of your travels, and news from across the desert."

"Yes, sir," came Nazir's reply to the command.

The great hall was filled with the remaining residents of the village who gathered around the young man now seated on cushions in the middle of the room. The dinner, which consisted of goat's cheese, fruits and nuts, was served by young children who stared in amazement at the warrior. The older boys muttered amongst themselves that he appeared not much older than they. They ate in awkward silence. Nazir was waiting for his host to initiate the conversation, but his hosts thought that they should let the boy eat in peace. There would be enough time for talking.

Sha Ram spoke first, "We are pleased that you are here, Nazir of the Shalaris. I know of your tribe. They are honorable and hospitable people. We welcome you once again to our house, and hope that our meager dinner was to your satisfaction."

"Thank you again, sir, for your kindness, hospitality and generosity. I am honored to be your guest," came Nazir's reply. The young boys realized instantly that this young man was no child. There was an air about him. They noted that he sat erect, shoulders pulled back, and a look of determination. The elders nodded sagely. They, too, instinctively knew that somehow this boy was different. Yes, he did have a boyish face and charm, but there was something else about him – something mysterious and deep, but yet not alarming. Once again, there was silence. Everyone was waiting.

Sha Ram motioned to Nazir, "Now, you shall tell us of your adventures, White Fire."

Nazir was thunderstruck. "How did he know?" he thought to himself. Who is this man that he could see into my mind? There was a sharp intake of breath followed by whispers among the elders, who were equally surprised. After all, this was the great Sha Ram, they thought. Anything is possible.

Nazir started to speak but could only manage, "But, how did you know...?"

"It is written in your eyes and your heart," came the reply. "And, the stick with the eyes of the snake – your protector. You are the White Fire."

Nazir could only reply, "Yes, sir, I am the White Fire."

With those words, everyone in the room fell forward, touching their foreheads to the ground in a show of deep respect. The nearest elder reached for the hem of Nazir's robe. This was the White Fire, the savior they had so long hoped would come to rescue them from the clutches of the evil that had befallen them and their village.

Nazir was overwhelmed. Not more than a short time ago, he was a humble member of his own tribe struggling to find his place with his people, but now he was the White Fire, Zoltan's warrior on a mission to rescue Amira, retake the Stone of Azurat – and save mankind in the process. The sight of a room full of people with their faces to the floor signaling their respect and devotion to him – to him – was more than he could take.

He spoke again. "Yes, my friends, I am the anointed one, the White Fire, but I am no more than a simple nomad like you. I did not seek this mantle, but I have accepted this responsibility to defeat Haroda, and rescue us all. And that I shall do for all of us; that is my destiny. I ask only this: that you help me to find her, for I do not know where to begin to search for the evil witch."

Almost as one, the faces turned to Sha Ram. They knew the answer to Nazir's request, but it would be for Sha Ram to speak, to make good on the request of the White Fire. Sha Ram was their leader, but they knew that he also had the most to lose in responding to Nazir's request. They knew that the answer to the White Fire's request lay with Jamila, Sha Ram's only child, his beloved daughter.

The leader looked around at the faces imploring him for his response. Sha Ram always knew in his heart that this day would come. He knew that the key to Haroda's defeat would be Jamila. He realized that her whole life was a preparation for this moment, that her destiny was about to intersect with that of the White Fire. It was now to be their combined destiny. It troubled him deeply, but he knew that Jamila had an equal part to play in the forthcoming battle between good and evil. The White Fire could not accomplish his task without her. Jamila was all that the leader had left in life. Her mother had died of a sickness when Jamila was a baby. She was his only joy. He could only manage laughter when he watched her playing with the other children in the village.

He sighed, then turned to one of the elders, and with a somber voice, said, "Call Jamila."

A few moments passed without a sound. Sha Ram's heart was heavy. A terrible sadness had come over his face. From the back of the large hall, a young woman began making her way forward. "Yes, father, here I am." With that, Sha Ram's face lit up. There she was – his beloved Jamila. She was beautiful beyond words. Her skin was a lustrous brown, and long black curls fell down to her shoulders. Her green eyes were gentle, and like her father, piercing. She walked erect and proud. As she walked toward her father in the inner circle, the children took her hand and the hem of her robe. They loved her as an older sister, as a playmate, and as a friend. Her smile was evidence of deep compassion. Like her father, it was clear that she was a very special person, and like the White Fire seated in front of her, one also destined to do great things.

Nazir was transfixed. He had never seen someone so beautiful. In her white robe, she was like a vision. *No*, he thought, *words cannot do her justice.* Nazir stood up to greet her. He spoke first but could hardly string three simple words together. "Er…I am…er… Nazir," he fumbled.

She smiled gently, and nodded her head to acknowledge the greeting. "I am Jamila, daughter of Sha Ram of Jabhar. Welcome."

"Sit my child. Sit next to me. Here before us is the expected White Fire. He is about to tell us of his adventures," said Sha Ram gesturing for her to sit between him and Nazir. Sha Ram looked at Nazir, and with a wave of his hand, said, "Nazir, White Fire, tell us; tell us how you came to be here in Jabhar."

And with that, Nazir began to recount his amazing journey. Nazir told his audience about the sandstorm that overcame him at the encampment of his tribe. What started as a walk to the well to fetch water for his mother had turned out to be a voyage to the outer reaches of Galthoram. He told the elders how he had wandered the dead landscape of the Zunir, his chance meeting with Gaius Fortus, who told him of his identity and destiny as the White

Fire, the Cave of Sorrows, and the epic battles with the Craxon and the Valerian Warlocks. His audience listened, captivated. Truly, this was the White Fire. One of the elders spoke, "White Fire, what has become of Gaius Fortus? Surely, you saved him from the fate of eternal damnation in the Zunir?"

Nazir explained that only the purest of the pure – the White Fire - could escape from the Zunir and pass through the Cave of Sorrows, and then only with the aid of the snakehead staff, his protector and connection to the gods who appointed him to this mission. He held up the stick to the elders. Immediately, the snake's yellow eyes began to glow. The old men shrunk back in terror. "Have no fear, my friends, this staff will not harm you; it protects me from Haroda's treachery. This is both my shield and my sword. With it, I am the arm of Zoltan. We shall defeat her, restore the Earth, and bring peace to all the land. When I complete this sacred mission, I will return to that forsaken place to rescue my friend and teacher, Gaius Fortus. This, I promise. It is my destiny."

Again, there was a long silence as each of the elders considered what they had just heard. They remembered Nazir's request, "I ask only this: that you help me to find her, for I do not know where to begin to search for the evil witch." However, the elders already knew the answer. Sha Ram knew the answer, but there was only one person who could take up that request: Jamila. No one spoke, for no one wished to offer her name.

Jamila knew what they were thinking. "I will help you, White Fire," she said simply.

Nazir started to object, "I thank you for your courage, Jamila, but..."

"White Fire, I know where Haroda can be found. I am the only one who can lead you there," she said matter-of-factly.

Nazir sensed that this young woman was not asking, but stating what everyone else in the room already knew. She was the key to finding Haroda. He also had the feeling that she was not a person who would easily be put off once she had made up her mind. The young warrior was fascinated.

"How do you know this?" Nazir asked.

"I was there," came the simple response.

Nazir could only stare in disbelief. *She was there? How? Why? And she survived?* The thoughts kept flooding in.

Jamila knew what he was thinking. She looked at her father. He took a deep breath and nodded his approval, knowing what was about to come next. It saddened him greatly that she would have to put herself through the torture of reliving such an experience, but they both knew that it was necessary – now more than ever. The young princess frowned momentarily as she began the tale of her horrific journey to Galthoram...

CHAPTER 11

Jamila

It was a beautiful day in Jabhar. The market was teeming with desert travelers buying goods for their onward journey. The little children of Jabhar played by the clear water flowing gently from a statue of the Goddess Amira. Under the watchful eye of their mothers, they splashed each other and occasionally their mothers as they ran in and out of the pool that formed under the waterfall. They laughed, giggled and screamed in delight. One child, however, stood apart from the others, because she was under the watchful eye of a man. She was Jamila, the daughter of Sha Ram, the princess of the village, and the sole child of the village leader.

Jamila's mother had died from a fever. The little girl's days were spent sitting with her father as he conducted the business of the village. He rarely let her play with the other children by herself. His wife had died alone in their home while he was in the great hall. There were no goodbyes, no time to reconcile any differences or put their lives in order. He came home one evening to find Jamila sitting by her mother's bedside. "Father, is Mama sleeping? I can't wake her." He had lost his wife, but he would not lose his precious Jamila. No, she must be with him at all times; he would not make that mistake twice.

On rare occasions, Sha Ram would come to the Amira fountain to let Jamila play with the other children. He sat by himself and watched her every move. It was only then that he could hear her laugh with her playmates. It made his heart leap for joy to see her jump in and out of the pool, racing round and round with the other children. In between her squeals, she would call out, "Father, father watch me. I can swim!" She got on her tummy in the shallowest part of the pool, and pretended to be swimming – her arms and legs flailing. He laughed with her, and for those few moments, the joy of his daughter overcame his sadness. "Yes, Jamila, yes you can."

So it was during those early years that Jamila spent her days sitting with her father listening to the village elders discuss and debate the issues of the day – and learning as no child could. She could hear the other children playing, but she could only have a fleeting glimpse. Her life was by her father's side. Secretly, she too feared that if she left to play with the other children, her father would be gone as quickly as her mother. Father and daughter were inseparable, and they were happy.

One day, during the height of the summer heat, when all the villagers did no more than sit by the many pools and all work ceased, Jamila asked her father's permission to play with the other children at the fountain of Amira. "Please, Father, oh please, may we go? It is cool and wet, and fun, and..."

"All right, all right, child," he smiled at her enthusiasm. "Yes, let us go to the fountain."

Sha Ram sat with other men, sullen and uncomfortable having to accompany their wives and children to the fountain. They thought that men should be at the business of the village – trading, meeting with passing nomadic tribes, and discussing matters of great weight – not babysitting. One of the senior members of the tribal council grumbled, "Sha Ram, this day is for conducting business, not doing woman's work. Let us go to the great hall. There is much to discuss. The forthcoming visit of the tribe of Oxar, next year's crop planting, and the expansion of the village. Come."

"Go, my friends, begin the meeting. I wish to watch Jamila and the children. I have so little opportunity. They grow so quickly," he replied.

"But we cannot begin without our esteemed leader," came the reply from one of the men who knew full well that Sha Ram could not refuse.

Sha Ram looked over at his daughter, and then back at the other village elders, and then again at Jamila, torn between his duty and his beloved daughter. "Very well, let us go if it is that important."

He would live to regret that decision for the rest of his life.

"Please, dear ladies, look after my Jamila. I shall return within the hour." With that, he turned to the elders and left, but not before throwing a backward glance at his daughter, who had stopped to look at her father walking away. She thought it strange that her father would be leaving without saying anything to her. She, too, would remember that moment for the rest of her life.

A few minutes after the men disappeared into the great hall for their meeting, the sky suddenly turned black as night. The birds stopped singing, and the air became completely still. Darkness settled on the village like a blanket. It was suffocating. Everyone stopped and searched the sky for a sign. The silence was unsettling. It seemed as if the gurgling of the Amira fountain had been silenced. The children had stopped and searched the faces of their mothers for a sign. Then without warning, she appeared from behind the darkest of clouds: Haroda. The evil witch of Galthoram was surrounded by thousands upon thousands of giant black birds – each one was the same bird but with the power of Haroda's magic, the bird could multiply itself in an instant to appear to be thousands. This was the power of Siwa, the dreaded, merciless black falcon who preyed upon innocent mortals. The Siwa was an enormous black bird of prey with large wings that spread fifty feet on either side of its hideous head and razor-sharp beak. The talons of the vicious beast could easily tear a cow apart with one stroke. The terrifying beast would do

Haroda's malicious bidding without question, or hesitation.

The people in the village were paralyzed. They were powerless against the might of Haroda. "You, the people of Jabhar, refused to bow before me. Now you shall pay for your defiance." With a wave of her hand, the army of blackbirds descended on the village, and in one pass, picked up all the children of the village, including Jamila. "These are now mine, and without your children, this village will wither and die like fruits parched for water in the desert sun," Haroda called down. The giant birds, each with a child in their claws, disappeared into the clouds. From that moment on, the village of Jabhar began its decline into utter desolation.

Hearing the shrieks from the Siwa, Sha Ram and the elders ran from the great hall in time to see all the village children being carried off into the clouds. The evil witch flew from her perch in the clouds to the center of the village square, "Sha Ram, kneel before me, and I shall return them."

"Never shall I kneel before you, witch. Return these children in the name of Zoltan!" the leader shouted.

Haroda laughed. "You are a fool! Sha Ram, I have your precious Jamila. You shall never see her again."

Sha Ram's heart sank. He looked over to the Amira fountain; the mothers were clutched together, sobbing. *No, no, not Jamila. I lost my wife, now Jamila. Why are the gods so cruel? Have I not been loyal? Why?*

∞

Zoltan, the greatest of the gods, heard, but it was too late. Haroda had the children captive. He could do nothing. A great sadness overcame him, mixed with anger and resolve. He would put an end to Haroda. He would find a warrior hero whom he would anoint to pursue the evil one, and forever end her reign of terror, restore his own daughter, Amira, to the throne of Earth together with the Azurat.

∞

As time passed, the people of the village of Jabhar sunk deeper into despair. They had lost their children; the village itself had become a wasteland, and hope of recovery vanished like sand in the wind. The wells dried up; the fruits withered on the vines and died; and the fountain to Amira lay in ruins. It seemed as if the very village itself began to surrender to the ravages of despair, and to the desert winds. One by one, the villagers left Jabhar; some died of heartbreak. Despite his despondency over the loss of Jamila, Sha Ram kept a brave face for his people. He could not succumb. He had to be their strength. They looked to him for hope, comfort and strength. Time passed slowly and painfully. Those days were seared in his memory. Not a day passed that he didn't think about that fateful day when he lost his beloved Jamila.

∞

The children of Jabhar found themselves in the dimly lit chamber of a cave. The torches cast long shadows on the little children, making them appear like grotesque figures dancing in spasms. They were now huddled together – some were crying for their mothers – all of them frightened and trembling. A few moments ago, some of them were playing in the fountain while others were playing in the flower bed. Without warning, they found themselves in the clutches of the Siwa, and now, held captive by an evil witch in the dreaded Galthoram. Their older siblings had told them stories about witches and ghosts at bedtime. They took delight in scaring the little ones, as older children so often do. But this time, it was no bedtime story; it was real. They looked up to see the hideous Haroda and the black falcon – the Siwa – perched high on a stone. Its evil eyes looked down at them hungrily. Haroda screamed at them, condemning them to a life of slavery to her wishes.

The Siwa shrieked at them, threatening to tear them apart if they dared to defy his mistress.

Haroda then took a different turn. "My children," she cackled. "My children, you shall be my family. My dear little ones, I shall teach you, nurture you. The Siwa will protect you. No harm shall come to you."

"You are not our mother; you will never be our mother," one of the children shouted up to Haroda.

"Silence!" she screamed at the little girl whom she immediately recognized as Jamila. The little girl cowered for a moment, but then remembered that she was the daughter of Sha Ram; she was a princess. Jamila stood up in defiance at the witch, her eyes glaring with anger as she spoke.

"We are not your children; we will never be your family, evil witch."

Haroda shrieked, "You insolent dog. The Siwa will silence you." With that, the giant black falcon swooped down on Jamila, its talons extended for the kill. Jamila felt the searing pain and then nothing. The other children screamed in terror as they watched the falcon take the princess.

As Jamila slowly regained consciousness, she felt her arm burning as if on fire. At least she was alive, she thought, but any pleasant thoughts of survival were overcome with the awareness of where she was, and the pain in her arm. She was alone now – alone, that is, except for the Siwa that stood menacingly over her. She could hear the children in the distance crying. She looked around her and found herself lying in a pile of straw that was strangely comfortable, until she realized that she was in the Siwa's nest! In a corner, she saw the skeleton of a human being, but it was the voice she heard that made her cringe all the more.

"You are mine now. There is no escape. It is only the witch that stands between you and me, but I shall have you – just like him," came the deep and coarse voice of the Siwa, pointing its claw to the skeleton. She became even more aware of the pain in her arm. When she looked at the source of the pain, a cold wave of fear came over her. On her left shoulder was a large burn in the shape of a black falcon. At that moment, she looked up to see the large black wing of the black falcon coming at her. It struck her full force and sent her falling backward and unconscious.

At first, it sounded like a voice calling from a distance, "Princess, Princess Jamila." It was not the threatening voice of the Siwa. This distant whisper was softer, almost gentle. "Jamila, wake up. I am here to help you." Slowly, she opened her eyes, almost afraid to see what vision Haroda had conjured up this time. She saw a kindly man kneeling over her. He had very long hair, dark eyes and a beard. In his hand, he clutched a staff with what looked like the head of the snake on the knob end. The young girl shrunk back in fear; she could trust no one.

"It's all right, my child. I am not one of them. I will not hurt you. I am Gaius Fortus," the man said, hoping to soothe the frightened girl who stared at him wide-eyed.

"What... what do you want?" she stammered, still reeling from the blow of the Siwa.

"We must hurry, child. We must get the other children and escape before more harm comes to all of you, especially you, Jamila."

"But, how do you know my name, Gaius Fortus?"

"That is not important now. The witch and that monster bird are not here. Now is our time," the bearded man said. "We must go. Please, Princess. Let us find the other children."

Jamila struggled to get to her feet, and as she did so, exposed her arm. Gaius Fortus saw the black falcon of the Siwa on the girl's arm and recoiled in horror. "You have been marked, my child," he exclaimed

"Yes, I see, and it burns," she replied.

The man replied, "Do you know what this means?" Without waiting for her reply, the man spoke again, "It is a curse that means the beast knows where you are at all times. The Siwa can sense the mark on your arm. It will find you wherever you are; there is no hiding. The only way to elude this monster is to never expose your arm to the light. For the rest of your life, your arm must remain covered." The only other way is for the Siwa to be killed by the gods or their appointed champion. Jamila quickly covered her arm despite the pain the cloth caused when it came in contact with her burning skin.

Jamila and Gaius Fortus climbed down from the Siwa's lair into the caves to make their way to the children. All was silent. The man was right, she thought. Both the evil witch and her black bird were away, probably bringing misery to another village or to an unwary tribe. She means to subjugate all mankind to her will.

They found the children huddled together. Some were sleeping from the sheer exhaustion of their ordeal; others were too frightened to sleep, and some seemed to be in a trance so great was their shock. Now, all they had to do was to gather the children, escape Haroda and the Siwa, and find their way back to Jabhar. The next days would be very long and dangerous.

Gaius Fortus had risked his own life to help them escape the evil witch and her black bird. His plan was elegant in its simplicity. With the aid of his magic stick with the snakehead, he created an optical illusion of the children still clutching each other in fear of the queen of the witches. It was only hours later when the Siwa retreated to its lair and discovered that Jamila was not in the nest, that the deception was uncovered. At that instant, the illusion disappeared. There was nothing; the children had fled. Haroda flew into an uncontrollable rage. "Who has dared to do this? Who dares defy me?"

At the entrance to Haroda's cave, Gaius put his hand on Jamila's shoulder and said to her, "I cannot go any further. It is my curse. Jamila, you do not have the benefit of waiting to become a leader. You must lead them now. These children are in your hands." With that, the magician pointed to a spot on the desert horizon and said, "Go now, Princess. Hurry. Travel only by day and in absolute silence. Haroda will not be able to hear, and the Siwa is blind in daylight. At night, you must take care to hide. Cover yourselves with sand and keep absolutely still." She looked first into the distance at the spot to which the magician had pointed and then at the children. When she turned to thank the man, he had disappeared.

∞

The sun was high in the sky; the sand dunes looked like waves on the sea that stretched beyond the horizon. The little ones were terrified of Haroda and Siwa. They held hands and kept silent as they trudged and stumbled their way across the fierce and desolate desert. After an exhausting trek that seemed never-ending, one of the children saw in the distance the vague outline of a village and whispered, "Look, Jamila, can it be? Is that our home? Is it Jabhar?"

The young girl was alone in her thoughts as she led the rag-tag group of children to freedom.

"Jamila, is that our village?" the child asked again.

She snapped out of her daydream. Not wanting to discourage the children, but wanting to be honest about the danger that lay ahead of them, she turned to the group and said, "I don't know children, I hope it is. If not, we must not be disheartened. We have each other; we must be brave. We will find home soon." Shielding her eyes, she peered into the distance seeing only shimmering waves of heat rising off the dunes. The desert nomads called this phenomenon Shalarian. No, there was no village. It was a mirage. These were hallucinations brought on by exposure to the intense heat of the desert and lack of water. It had brought grief to many a traveler.

On the first night of their travels, remembering Gaius Fortus' advice, they covered themselves over in the sand. They remained absolutely still and silent, except for the muffled crying of several of the youngest children. While overhead, the Siwa circled the night sky in its relentless but vain attempt to find them. As the sun broke the horizon, the Siwa was forced to retreat to the Galthoram. "I shall find them, especially the princess, and devour them all. There will be no escape." the Siwa said aloud.

Another day, another challenge to stay alive. They were now completely alone and relying only on the determination of Jamila. She had to lead them to safety, into the arms of their mothers, and to reunite with her beloved father, Sha Ram. For three days, they walked across the vast desert without food and little water under the brutal sun. On the morning of the third day, after brushing off the sand, one of the children, the youngest, began to cry and, between sobs, whispered, "We are going to die. We will never see our families."

Jamila reached out to the little girl and held her. "Don't be sad, little one, just a little longer, and I promise you that you will be with your mother." She leaned over and kissed the child, who wiped away her tears and forced a smile.

Jamila brought the group into a tight circle. "Courage everyone. We are almost there. Remember, silence. We do not want her and that ugly bird to hear us."

After a long and grueling day in the blistering heat, at last, there it was – home. Yes, she could just see the outline of the familiar towers. "Look children, there. See! We are home!" Forgetting the need for silence, the excited children broke into chatter, laughter, and shouts of joy. Jamila was momentarily horrified. Haroda and the Siwa would certainly have heard them. "Children let us hurry."

Despite the heat and thirst, the children broke into an open run toward the gates of the village. The sentry saw the tattered group of children led by Jamila, who stood covered in a white robe standing tall. He rubbed his eyes, hardly believing what he was seeing. No, it was not an illusion; it was real! He shouted down to the other villagers, "They have returned to us! They have returned – our children!" Within seconds, the large wooden gate of the village was thrown open. Mothers and fathers poured out to embrace their children, smothering them with hugs and kisses. Jamila, the princess, stood there alone for a few moments watching families being reunited. She searched the faces for the one she wanted to see most: Sha Ram. When she saw him, he was standing there alone watching her, studying her, admiring his daughter – proud of her courage and leadership. She rushed into his arms, nearly knocking him over. "Father, dearest father, I missed you so. For a time, I thought I would never see you again. I thought I would die." With that, for the first time, she let herself feel the fear, the anxiety, the loneliness and the pressure of assuming the role of the leader. She buried her head into her father's shoulder and cried.

Father and daughter walked back into the village to the cheers of the villagers. "You did well, my dearest Jamila. You did well. I, no *we*, are so proud of you! We are indebted to you, child. Hear them? They are celebrating the return of their children, and your heroism, Jamila."

CHAPTER 12

The White Fire and Jamila

"...And so, White Fire, you see this is why I must accompany you," she concluded simply and calmly.

All eyes turned to the White Fire. The young man was stunned. What could he say? He had never heard of such courage and virtue before. This young woman seated in her long white robe at the council of elders was devoted to her father, her village, and its long-suffering people. She had risked her life, and was prepared to risk it again. He thought to himself that only until recently, he had spent his young life sheltered by his mother and his tribe. It was only after he had been anointed to be the White Fire did he confront all the horrors of the evil that surrounded him, and the dangers involved in his quest. On the other hand, this young woman, he thought, had come face to face with death at tender years, and demonstrated the purity of spirit and a selfless desire to protect her village.

And then, it came to him like a sandstorm rolling down a desert valley. *Is it possible? Can there be more than one? No, it cannot be; she is one who has already done her share of the conflict with the evil spirits. But then, does that matter? She is pure of spirit; blameless and committed to mankind, and prepared to risk herself in a noble cause.* He searched her eyes, trying to find the answer. He looked around him, hoping that some disembodied voice would answer the question. Jamila looked at him with a gentle, knowing smile. She knows what I am thinking! Without taking his eyes off her, Nazir walked over to her with his snakehead staff. Slowly, he raised it in her direction. The snake's eyes began to glow a bright yellow.

"Al haber, al asham – Tell me. Can there be two White Fires?"

Instantly, there was a burst of the brightest white light. The elders were momentarily blinded and threw themselves on their faces in terror. From inside the fiery white light came a thundering voice.

"Although there can be but one who is anointed as the White Fire, there are many who are equal in virtue and purity. Jamila is such a one. Trust her, for you cannot succeed in this quest without her."

Instantly, the white light disappeared. Nazir looked at Jamila, whose face resembled a tranquil pond. She smiled gently and said, "I always knew in my heart that this day would come, the day when our people – this world – would be freed from the scourge of Haroda. I give you my loyalty and commitment, White Fire. Together, we shall fulfill your destiny...and mine."

CHAPTER 13

The Siwa

Nazir and Jamila stepped through the gates of the village to see the vast expanse of the desert before their eyes. Jamila stopped and turned to look back. She saw the earnest and grave faces of the villagers who promised to pray for their safe return. In front of the group was Sha Ram. Jamila walked back, and threw her arms around him just as she had done so many times before, and whispered in his ear, "I love you, Father. I shall return." With that, she walked back to stand beside Nazir. "I am ready, White Fire."

The village leader remained, looking into the distance long after the two young warriors had disappeared over the dunes. He took a long, deep breath, and held it for a moment. He then turned around, released his breath, and stepped back over the threshold. "Close the gate," he ordered.

Jamila and Nazir walked for days in the blistering heat, stopping only briefly at night to rest for several hours. When they did speak, it was only in a hushed whisper. He had responded to the caution relayed to Jamila by Gaius Fortus years earlier: travel only during the day as the Siwa is blinded by daylight, do not speak for Haroda will hear and cover yourselves at night with sand lest the Siwa find you. "Al haber, al asham – Shield us from view." Instantly, except for their footfalls in the sand, they became invisible.

One night, as they sat under the stars, Nazir broke the long silence as he sat with his knees against his chest. "This is my favorite time. I see my father in the stars. The night sky is deep and comforting. I feel...," he hesitated, searching for the right word, "joy." They then covered themselves with sand and promptly fell into a deep sleep. Unbeknownst to them, high above, the Siwa was searching for any unsuspecting victim. The beast could not know, but the snakehead staff, with its fierce yellow eyes, scanned the night sky, watching the big bird circling the night sky.

On the fourth night, as they sat alongside one another, exhausted from trudging in the scorching desert sun, Nazir turned to Jam ila and offered her water, some dried fruit, and bread. She waved it away and said, "You should eat first, White Fire. You will need all your strength." Her kindness and compassion moved him. "Perhaps I am the White Fire, but if there could be two, I believe that you would be the other," Nazir said simply.

In the dim light of the moon, Jamila looked at the young warrior. His face was young and handsome, but there was a look of fierce determination as well. His dark eyes were like white-hot coals. Except for the occasional glance to see if she was keeping up with his furious pace, he kept his focus on the horizon. He knew – indeed they both knew – that this would be the final battle. There could only be one winner, and for him, losing was not an option. It was his destiny, and now hers as well, to rescue the Goddess Amira and retrieve the Azurat – the key to the earth. He spoke rarely, not for fear that Haroda would hear them, but because there was not much to say.

They walked in silence for the remainder of the fifth day. The sun and the sky turned a brilliant orange as dusk approached. Ahead of them lay a lone, scraggy mountain that seemed to rise abruptly from the desert floor. It seemed out of place, like a dark blot on an otherwise vast desert plain. In fact, to Nazir, it did not look real. It was as if one of the gods had piled stones one atop the other as a marker to find the same spot on a return journey, but at the same time, it struck him as ominous. He stopped to study it further, but Jamila filled in the blank for him.

"White Fire, there it is: the entry to Galthoram, the home of Haroda. We must be careful."

But it was too late. Although they were invisible, the evil witch heard them. She could hear the beating of their hearts. "So, he comes – the White Fire – this boy, arrogant enough to think he can defeat me, Haroda, Queen of Galthoram. And he brings with him that wench who escaped from us. I will show them no mercy. They shall both die."

She summoned the Siwa from his lair within the mountain cave. "My beloved raven, do not fail me. The night approaches, and they will need to sleep. You are master of the night. Find them, and kill them both," she commanded.

"Yes, my queen," came the hoarse-throated reply. The black bird's eyes burned with vengeance. Yes, he would kill the White Fire, but first, he would have the woman who traveled with him, the woman who had outwitted him years ago. She was going to be his prize. The bird leaped into the air, and within seconds flew into the night sky. This time, she would not escape.

Nazir replied to Jamila's urging for caution by showing her the wooden snakehead staff with the eyes now glowing a bright yellow. "Yes, princess. You are right. My guardian staff senses the danger as well. See his eyes begin to glow."

Slowly and cautiously, they moved around the dunes to get closer to the jagged mountain. "I think we should stop and rest for the night. We are both tired. We will be protected by the staff." Jamila agreed. It was the first time they had stopped that day. They had been pushing themselves to their physical limits for the past several days, and they knew that they would need all their strength to engage Haroda and her legions of evil creatures. Nazir offered Jamila some food, as they had not eaten for over a day, but she, too, was too exhausted to take any more than a cupful of water. Nazir held up the staff, "Al haber, Al asham, cloak us in invisibility from Haroda's minions." Immediately, an invisibility screen surrounded the duo. It would protect from Haroda and the beasts under her command. Within minutes, they were both fast asleep, not taking the precaution of covering themselves with sand, satisfied that the invisibility cloak would protect them. They had not noticed a bird that was making endless circles high above them, waiting for the moment to strike.

Nazir slept fitfully. His dreams were invaded by fire-breathing dragons attacking him, Haroda screaming curses, and loud voices urging him to fulfill his destiny to save the world. His arms swung and lashed out at the imaginary monsters with his snakehead staff. In his dream sleep, he was fighting a losing battle – the more he slew, the more that rose against him. It was in the course of one of these dream skirmishes that he slashed at his enemy with his snakehead staff. He beat back hordes of the evil beasts. The monsters in his dreams were defeated, but the staff flew out of Nazir's grasp. In his sleep, he could not have remembered the stern warning of Gaius Fortus, "Do not release the staff from your grasp. Without it, you are as vulnerable as any other human being." The staff fell several feet away from the sleeping young warrior, but in his sleep, he could not know that the shield of invisibility had disappeared. At that very instant, the cloak disappeared, and the Siwa saw his prey lying peacefully asleep.

The black raven tucked in his wings, and began a nearly vertical dive. Its fierce eyes were completely focused on Jamila. It covered the nearly mile-high distance in seconds, so great was the Siwa's speed and determination to make the kill. Like a bomb falling from the sky, the bird's descent sounded like a high-pitched scream. From somewhere in his dream sleep, Nazir heard the incoming bird, but by the time his unconscious mind covered the distance between dreaming and waking, the Siwa struck. The bird's wings were at full span as it braked long enough to grab hold of the sleeping Jamila. Nazir awoke in time to see the talons take hold of the young woman. Half awake, half asleep, he tried to comprehend what was happening. In that instant, the Siwa struck him full force with one of its wings, propelling Nazir into the air like a discarded toy. He landed unconscious.

∞

As Jamila regained consciousness – even before she opened her eyes, she instantly knew where she was. She remembered the stench, and it made her vomit.

"Well, not so tough, are we, **Princess** Jamila," the Siwa sneered, emphasizing the word "princess."

She tried to get to her feet to stand in defiance of the creature, but she was too bruised and beaten by her ordeal. She stumbled forward. She remained on her hands and knees for a long time, trying desperately to recover. Her long black hair was matted and hung in front of her eyes. Her head hurt - probably when the bird dropped her onto the cave floor. She could taste the blood that dripped down her face into her mouth. There was blood on her arms and legs. Her white robe was in shreds and covered in blood.

"You shall die, woman, but only when I choose. First, you shall feel the pain of my talons, and perhaps worse, you shall know the feeling of helplessness. There is no one this time to save you. You are mine to dispose of." The Siwa spoke his words slowly, and in a low growl to affect the maximum pain on Jamila.

At that moment, she no longer cared whether she lived or died; perhaps it was better to die than to endure the pain and cruelty of this beast. Perhaps, this was her destiny, but then, it slowly came to her, *"No, this cannot be. I do not fear death, but death at the hands of this creature cannot be my fate."* Struggling with every ounce of her might, she raised herself to her feet. She looked up at the Siwa – into its fierce black eyes with an equal fierceness that even surprised the monster - "Go to hell."

∞

He did not know how long it had been since he was unconscious – a day, perhaps – maybe more. Slowly, it was all coming back to him, faster and faster. He and Jamila were asleep; he dreamed; then he remembered the whistling sound, then the Siwa, and then nothing. He looked around him. He saw Jamila's blanket. It was covered in blood. Slowly, he got to his feet; nothing was broken, just a headache from being slapped by the Siwa's black wing. Then it struck him. "My staff. Where is my staff?" He looked around him. There was nothing but the remnants of the attack. He began to panic. Without that staff, how could he fulfill his mission? How would he find the strength? He dropped to his hands and knees, and began furiously clawing at the sand where he thought the snakehead staff might be. There was nothing. Then, as quickly as he panicked, a strange feeling came over him. This is not how the White Fire should behave, he thought. He stopped, stood up and composed himself. "I am the White Fire," he said softly aloud. "I cannot, will not, be deterred from my destiny."

He closed his eyes for a moment, and then opened them. He straightened his shoulders, and lifted his head. Again, he said – this time much louder - "I am the White Fire. I cannot, will not, be deterred from my destiny." He took a deep breath, and with firmness and determination in his voice, he said, "Al haber, al asham" – My staff and protector, come to me." With that, the sand around him swirled as if in a cyclone, and within an instant, the staff emerged from beneath the sand. The snake's eyes immediately filled the air with a fierce yellow glow. "Yes, my friend. Haroda shall not succeed. First, we go to find Jamila, and then we shall finish this business once and for all. Let us go."

CHAPTER 14

The Siwa vs. Jamila

The entrance to the cave at the base of the mountain was large and forbidding. At the mouth, there was a human skull and a sign: "ςωχ∇τƷ" ("**Beyond, there is no hope, no return**"). Immediately beyond the entrance, there was total darkness. Daylight was unable to penetrate beyond the threshold of the cave, such was the evil inside. Inside was the lair of the Siwa, where he would find Jamila, but it was also the entrance to Galthoram, the kingdom of the damned - the kingdom of the evil witch Haroda. Once inside, there was no return until victory or death. He stepped into the darkness. "Al haber, al asham – Give me light." The snake's yellow eyes immediately glowed like a lantern. The beam of light surrounded Nazir like a bubble.

The White Fire walked slowly, his every sense keen to any change in his surroundings. He peered to the limit of the yellow light provided by the snakehead. Beyond the light, there was total blackness. He could hear a low moaning sound, the sound of a person in agonizing pain, but unable to scream. It was the saddest sound he had ever heard. What could cause such sadness, he asked himself? He walked deeper into the cave,. Holding the snakehead in front of him, he measured each step, one foot in front of the other. He walked for hours, hearing only the constant moan of lost, suffering souls. Then, suddenly, another sound – different from the moaning...he stopped, straining to hear. It was not the inarticulate sound of the doomed...There it was again. Yes, it was a voice, deep and ominous. From within the depths of the cave, the sound became louder. He turned toward the direction and quickened his pace. The voice became louder still.

"There is no hope for you, Jamila, no one will come to rescue you. You shall die here alone. They have abandoned you."

"No, she is not alone, Siwa, and no, she will not die," came the voice of the White Fire as he stepped into the colossal chamber.

"Ahh," the Siwa shouted in shock and in anger. "You! You may have been able to defeat the Craxon and the Valerian Warlocks with your cheap magic tricks, but I am the Siwa, the greatest of them all. Today, you too shall die!" With that the Siwa flew from its perch, and streaked toward the White Fire.

"Al haber, al asham" – "Give me a sword." In a flash of yellow light, the snakehead staff produced a magnificent broad gold sword with a snake's head at the pommel end. The Siwa, however, was as clever as it was vicious. Seeing the sword materialize, it veered off, causing a great rush of wind to knock Nazir to the ground. Again, the black raven swooped low, but just out of reach of the White Fire, and again, with its wings pounding the air, it raised a cloud of dust that momentarily blinded the young man. Nazir's eyes were stinging. He lashed out with the enchanted sword, but could not see the bird. He slashed again and again at the empty air. In its third pass, the evil raven swooped down behind Nazir, and smacked him with its wing, knocking him to the ground again, sending the sword flying out of his hand.

The Siwa saw the opportunity for the kill. It came in fast, spread its large black wings, and extended its sharp talons. As the warrior rose to his feet, he saw the Siwa coming fast and low. With his reflexes sharpened from previous battles, he immediately dove to his right just at the instant the bird was about to impale him on one of its talons. However, the magical sword was just out of reach. He calculated that by the time he reached the special sword, this evil falcon was now making a sharp turn and heading straight toward him again, and would almost certainly have him. However, Nazir had no choice but to risk certain death to reach the staff. He feinted to the left, suggesting to the Siwa that he was going to run. At the very last second, he turned and lunged toward the staff. Now, firmly in his grasp, Nazir raised the snakehead staff to defend himself. "Al haber, al asham" – "Give me a shield." At the same moment the shield appeared, the raven hit him straight on. One of the talons pierced the shield, cutting the young man's arm and taking the shield with it still hanging from the talon. Again and again, the Siwa attacked, only to be denied as the White Fire eluded him with the help of the snakehead.

But the Siwa had miscalculated - it had lost sight of Jamila. It proved to be a fatal mistake.

As the raven kept up its relentless ground-level attack on Nazir, Jamila climbed down from the Siwa's perch in an effort to escape and to help the White Fire in the process. Mustering all her strength, she found Nazir's enchanted sword that had gone unnoticed by the monstrous bird. With the sword in hand, she dragged herself halfway back up to the Siwa's perch. With the whipping action of its wings, the black falcon kept up a constant barrage of stones that pelted the warrior like bullets fired from a gun. It slashed its talons in wide sweeps. Jamila looked down, and could see the Siwa closing the distance between it and Nazir.

This monster had tried to kill her and her friends when they were children. Now, it was about to do it again – to both her and the White Fire. She and Nazir were friends; he was the White Fire, and the gods had sent them on a quest to save the world. She was not going to permit this creature to stand between them and their mission. Her anger rose like bile from her stomach. "No more," she said aloud. "You will not kill or terrorize any longer. It stops here, now." With the strength that comes from fury, she raised the enchanted sword, pointed it downward, and threw herself off the ledge down thirty feet onto the back of the Siwa, who had at that moment heard Jamila shout, but it was too late. She landed on the falcon's back and, at the same time, plunged the sword deep into the base of the falcon's neck. The evil bird let out a piercing scream. It arched its back and flailed its wings in a vain attempt to dislodge the sword. Jamila was thrown to the ground. Nazir ran to her and pulled her behind a large stone. The Siwa screamed and cursed. Its talons slashed out in rage, but to no avail. The sword had done its work. The Siwa tried to scream once more, but nothing came from its throat. The look of shock and horror went out from the evil bird's eyes as it fell backward, dead, its black wings spread apart.

"Jamila, are you alright?" Nazir asked.

Jamila was sitting down, knees curled up to her chin, breathing heavily. She said nothing. She needed to let the rage pass, a feeling which until then was unknown to her.

"That was magnificent, Jamila. You are very brave. You risked your life for me. I shall forever be in your debt," was all that the young man could manage. He had no idea of the depth of the turmoil she was feeling at that moment. Never in her young life had she felt such extreme anger and hatred for anything. These feelings made her feel unclean and sick. Her stomach was turning; her breath came in giant heaves. When she did not reply, he understood that his own silence was the better course of action. He put his arm around her and sat alongside her. For a long time, neither of them spoke. After an hour passed, Nazir saw that Jamila had put her head on his shoulder and had fallen asleep.

Nazir looked at the sleeping young woman and was overcome with a strange feeling – something he never experienced. It was an odd feeling. He couldn't describe it, but it made him feel both happy and sad at the same time. The sight of her sleeping peacefully made him feel both strong and gentle. A brief smile crossed his face. She was so beautiful, he thought...

"White Fire?" she said as she opened her eyes.

"Yes, Jamila, I am here. It's finished. Thanks to you. The Siwa is dead, and we are safe for the moment. How are you feeling?"

She ached all over. She was covered in blood and bruises. Her clothes were in tatters. The young warrior understood. He took off his shirt and gave it to her.

"When you are ready, we will go," Nazir said softly.

"You are very kind, but we cannot wait. We must go now," Jamila said firmly as she painfully brought herself to her feet. "We must finish this. Besides, the evil witch must know that we are here, and that we have killed her beloved Siwa. She will want her revenge."

She walked over to the dead Siwa, and pulled the enchanted sword from the bird's neck. "I expect that we will need this."

With a mix of admiration and surprise, he looked at Jamila. He saw the determination in her eyes as she stood by the dead bird, sword in hand. He wondered who the real White Fire was. "Yes, I guess so."

CHAPTER 15

The Final Battle

Haroda stirred a pool of water with her gnarled hand and muttered, "Galana teesh." With that, the water boiled and turned into a mist. In the midst of the miasma, she saw and heard the battle between the two young warriors and the Siwa. She shrieked in horror as she witnessed the young woman drive the enchanted sword into the black falcon's neck killing it.

"Villains," she screamed. "Now, they must pay." Yet despite her efforts to thwart the White Fire with the Craxon, the Valerian Warlocks, and now the Siwa, she knew that the White Fire and his companion were drawing closer. She knew that the White Fire, together with Jamila, were determined to destroy her, rescue the Earth Goddess, and retrieve the Azurat that she wore around her neck. She felt for the stone to reassure herself that it still hung from her withered neck. No, she was not about to let these two impudent "children" wrest control over the Earth from her. The earth and all its miserable inhabitants were hers. The arid land was now an extension of the underworld, Galthoram. She was now queen of all that she surveyed. She must put a stop to them, and put an end to Zoltan's interference in her domain. But, for a brief moment, a wave of fear came over her. The White Fire had defeated both the Craxon and the Valerian Warlocks, and Jamila had destroyed Siwa. It was now or never.

Haroda turned nervously to look for him, the last line of defense. "Ricon, where are you?" she called out into the darkness of the caves. Her voice echoed off the walls that repeated her call over and over. Her voice finally faded into a whisper. Nothing. "Ricon!" she screamed. "Come to me." No sooner had she uttered the words when, out of the darkness, the monster burst into the chamber in a sulfurous explosion. Even for Haroda, the beast's features were unbearably ugly, and his ugliness was only exceeded by his ferocity and cruelty. Despite all her awesome power, cruelty and ruthlessness, she feared this creature. He was as likely to turn on her as any other. He had been condemned to the deepest and endless void of hell – the Lake of Eternal Fire - by Zoltan himself. Not even Haroda knew why. The misery and desolation of the deepest pit of hell made him the most fearsome of all the creatures of the underworld.

Ricon emerged from the inferno that was reserved only for him, the most wicked and cruel of beings.

"Why do you call, woman," he bellowed, his fierce eyes red and blazing with hatred and anger. His voice was like the explosion of a volcano; he spit fire and molten stones as he spoke. The large fangs in his mouth dripped with poison.

Haroda had not seen the beast in many years, but every time she saw him, it made her shiver. He stood thirty feet high with a scaly, black and red serpentine body. He had a human head with two giant, curved horns. The hideous beast had long arms, much like an octopus, that were covered in sharp spikes. At the tail end was an enormous barb that could cut a person in half. His entire body was poisonous. A touch from any part of him meant a horrible and agonizing death.

"Zoltan has sent a warrior to destroy us, Ricon – both of us," Haroda said, sounding braver than she really felt.

"Destroy **us**? You are a fool, woman. Destroy **us** to what end? I am already in the deepest pit of this hell."

He stopped for a moment, and slithered closer to the witch who, at the sight of him approaching her, took a step backward. That was a mistake. The Ricon sensed Haroda's fear, her uncertainty in the face of the White Fire and him. He sneered, "So, Zoltan sends a mere boy and girl to unseat you, woman. But this is not about me, is it? No longer shall you be the Queen of Galthoram, of this miserable earth, and all its wretched inhabitants." The Ricon loomed over Haroda, whose back was now pressed against the cave wall. His searing, hate-filled eyes penetrated the witch's heart.

"Ah, woman. You are afraid - afraid of the Ricon, of Zoltan, and of this White Fire and his companion," the Ricon continued his scornful reply. "They are not here to defeat me, witch. It is you they seek. You are doomed. Perhaps you shall spend your eternity in the Eternal Lake of Fire with me. That is your fear. Is it not?" The Ricon's fiery voice nearly overcame Haroda, but she was not ready to surrender. She summoned her outrage and her courage.

"Ricon, if I am defeated, what then? What shall happen to your fiery abode? Do you think that the queen of the Earth – the favorite of Zoltan – will ever permit the inhabitants of Earth to be damned to your fiery domain? She will protect them all, and in so doing, deny you the condemned souls that you so earnestly need to stoke your fires, and to satisfy your appetite for flesh."

The monster reared back and arched his back as if to strike the witch for her insolence. Through his dripping fangs, he roared through his pungent breath, nearly overcoming Haroda. "No one, not Amira, Zoltan, or any of the gods, can ever deny me the humans. They are weak: they kill, start wars with each other, cheat, and steal. Can any of the gods change what is in the nature of these pitiful humans? No, never! These miserable creatures even defy the gods' every attempt to help. I shall always have my fill."

Haroda found her opening. "Perhaps, Ricon, but the gods, Zoltan, in particular, have been moved by the White Fire, by the young princess Jamila – by their courage. They are now disposed to them, to help them defeat me, save the earth, and forever seal the dark world. The gods shall come here to prove their loyalty to Zoltan. You cannot defeat all of them. You know, Ricon, they will come to the defense of the White Fire. Only together will we be able to defeat them." She was lying, of course. The Ricon knew that the gods would not dare venture into Galthoram, and even if they could, they were powerless to help.

The Ricon hesitated. He knew that no one was a match against him, but an army of gods to support the White Fire would be too large a force even for such a formidable foe as Ricon. The monster fell silent. He slithered to the opposite wall of the cave, coiled himself, and for many moments, was absolutely still, all the while keeping one eye trained on the witch. Haroda remained frozen in her spot; she dared not move.

"Very well, woman, I shall protect you," the words came like tongues of fire from the Ricon.

"Good. They are here in the cave, in the upper chambers. They seek to free the Goddess, Amira."

"Well, then, we shall let them find her. Bring Amira to this chamber. We shall make quick work of this White Fire," commanded the Ricon.

"Yes, my lord Ricon," the witch replied deferentially.

Within a few moments, Haroda reappeared with the most beautiful woman known to both man and the gods – Amira. Despite her captivity in a deep pit with neither food nor water, the Goddess looked radiant, reflecting not only her outer beauty, but also her inner peace and tranquility. Her white robe was in tatters, and stained with mud, but she stood serenely above the insanity that surrounded her.

The Ricon was intrigued by the stillness that she radiated despite his threatening demeanor. "Do you know who I am, woman?"

"Yes, I know who you are, Ricon," she said quietly.

"Are you not afraid?"

"No, Ricon, I am not. I am filled with sorrow and pity for you condemned as you are. I shall ask my father, Zoltan..."

At the mention of his name, the Ricon reared back, preparing to strike the Queen of Earth, and then bellowed, "Zoltan! It is he who created me, and he who condemned me to this place. Why? For the sole reason that I might torture those souls who refused to do his will. And you. You were created to glorify him. The only difference between us is the hazy line between good and evil. We both sprang from the same god. That would make us brother and sister, woman."

"Yes, we are all brothers and sisters. I bear you no ill will, Ricon. I shall intercede with him for you," Amira said gently.

The Ricon stopped, surprised by her simple kindness. He let it pass just as quickly. Between his poisonous fangs, he sneered, "Well, then, sister, you shall be both witness and victim. Today, we destroy this White Fire, after which it shall be your turn to feel the pain of torture and death – in satisfaction of the misery visited upon me by **our** father, Zoltan," he spat with emphasis on "our".

With that, the Ricon turned to Haroda and commanded, "Woman, chain her to the wall."

Nazir and Jamila continued their slow downward journey into the depths of the Galthoram. Neither spoke, but both knew that their fate could be decided with the next footfall. Nazir held the snakehead staff, from which emanated a yellow glow much like a lantern. In the distance, they could hear what sounded like thunder. As they got closer, the thunder became a rumble, and then louder still – a growl that echoed off the black walls of the pathway. They continued on the sloping path deeper into the abyss. Suddenly, the growl stopped. There was nothing but absolute silence. They could only hear the sound of the stones grinding under their boots; it was deafening. They stopped, too. Now, they could only hear the sound of their own breathing. The two warriors took several steps forward and suddenly found themselves in a cavernous hall. So large was this room that the yellow light disappeared into the upper reaches and the breadth of this space.

"Keep close to the wall," Nazir whispered. "I fear we would be easy prey in the open."

They moved slowly, carefully keeping their backs against the wall. They were nearly overcome with the heat and the sulfurous stench. The heat was like a furnace, greater than the open desert at the height of the day. The disgusting odor was that of rot and death. Jamila stifled a gag, and Nazir put his free hand to his mouth and nose. Ahead of them in the dim yellow light, they could barely make out the outlines of what appeared to be a person, a woman. She had her back against the wall, and her arms were spread eagle. At hearing them, the woman in chains turned to look at them. She was saying something and shaking her head, but they could not hear. They came closer.

Yes, it was a woman, but she was not dressed as any ordinary woman, and despite her ragged clothing, they could see her beauty. The woman again turned to them and was turning her head from side to side and seemed to mouthing the same word over and over, *"Go. No. Go."*

Nazir ran over to the woman. "My lady, who are you? How did you get here?"

Jamila knew, "White Fire, it is Amira, Goddess of the Earth."

Both of the warriors fell to their knees and put their faces to the ground.

"Children, you must go. It is not safe; it is a trap for you, White Fire. Please, you must go," Amira said. Nazir and Jamila could sense both the urgency and the fear in her voice.

At that very moment, it became so clear to him – clear as the cool water in the pool of the oasis. Now was the moment of his destiny. It was here and now that his role in the clash between good and evil would be played out...to the death. His body began to quiver with both fear and excitement. He took a deep breath, and then slowly rose to face the Goddess.

"My lady, I am the White Fire. The gods have sent me to rescue you, and to recover the Azurat. And that is what I intend to do."

Amira looked at the proud young man who was prepared to sacrifice himself for her. She was moved by his courage, the purity of spirit, and his purposeful manner. So, this is why he was chosen. She thought to herself that the gods had chosen the perfect champion in Nazir, her White Fire. She was about to speak when suddenly the ground shook and the roar behind Nazir sent a wave of cold fear through him. The Ricon.

This was no ordinary monster. Nazir had fought so many in the past. How long had it been since he became the White Fire? Random and nonsense thoughts flooded his mind. He was instantly reminded of the other battles: Craxon, the sand dragon; the formless Volarian Warlocks, and the dreaded falcon, Siwa. How dangerous was this one? What evil does it possess? The Ricon's fangs were dripping with what had to be venom. He turned to face the beast to shield the Goddess. "No, Ricon, not today, not ever. She is the Goddess Amira, and it is my duty, my destiny, to protect her. I shall destroy you as I did the others."

"You fool. It is **YOU** I shall have," came the fierce reply. "And your pitiful companion, the princess Jamila. And then, I shall have the Goddess. I shall have all of you. And I shall start with you, you miserable wretch." And with that, the mighty Ricon reared back, bared his fangs, and struck out at the White Fire.

Fortified with the realization of his mission, and seeing his destiny in the flesh – the Goddess Amira – the boy, now a man, was ready to take the battle to the enemy. No longer would he defend. He would attack.

"Al haber, al asham - Give me a shield." The Ricon's strike fell onto a large golden shield that immediately materialized and covered the three intended victims. The Ricon reared back and struck again, but to no avail. The sound of its teeth on the cold metal shield reverberated in the chamber. Again and again, the Ricon reared and struck. It spit fire and poison; it slashed at the shield with its claws. Despite the Ricon's every attempt, the golden shield held.

Once again, the White Fire invoked the powerful snakehead staff, "Al haber, al asham" – Give me wings to fly." Instantly, enormous white wings came from between his shoulders. He sprung into the air as if catapulted. He flew high up to the vault of the chamber. The Ricon followed his every move, twisting round and round as White Fire circled like a hawk waiting to strike its prey. Faster and faster, the winged White Fire flew – so fast that he became a blur.

"Al haber, al asham - Give me a spear." Immediately, the snakehead staff became an enormous three-pronged spear, and with this trident spear, the White Fire struck the Ricon over and over as he flew in continuous circles at blinding speed. The White Fire struck him high, and then low, high again, low – over and over. The aerial attack went on for hours. The Ricon flailed at the White Fire like someone trying to swat a fly, but to no avail. The White Fire's strikes were relentless.

Ricon was bleeding profusely from the numerous blows, but his pain only fueled his anger and resistance.

On one high-speed pass by the White Fire, the Ricon's long nails clipped the warrior's wings, sending him tumbling in the air, and smashing into the cave wall. The Ricon saw his opportunity as the White Fire struggled to his feet and was about to launch himself into the air for another attack. The monster roared, "I have you now! Die!" The monster reared back, ready to strike the warrior with all his might. The creature was so focused on killing White Fire that he failed to notice the person creeping up to his side. Suddenly, Princess Jamila rushed forward, and plunged the magical sword that she had used to dispatch the Siwa, into the Ricon. The beast roared in pain from the enchanted sword that had cut deep into his side, and would certainly mean his imminent death. In a desperate attempt to have one last measure of revenge, the Ricon struck at the now-defenseless Jamila. Wounded and slowly dying, his fangs missed their mark, but his body brushed her arm. The glancing blow sent her tumbling forward, and crashing into the wall of the cave at the feet of the helpless Goddess. Jamila was knocked unconscious from crash, but the Ricon had succeeded in touching her, sending his poison coursing through her body.

"Jamila!" the White Fire shouted as he rushed over to her. She was still; her body was cold and bleeding. He turned to look up at the Ricon, who was wavering from the wounds he had received. It was clear to White Fire that Jamila had struck a fatal blow, but the beast was still dangerous.

"You may have sent me to my death, but I shall not go alone, White Fire. I shall take the two women with me. You shall be denied your destiny." Summoning all his remaining energy, the Ricon curled into a strike position, like a rattlesnake, and prepared himself to strike at the Goddess.

"Al haber, al asham - Give me a bow and a quiver of arrows." Standing in front of both the Goddess Amira and Jamila, the White Fire let loose with a thousand arrows in the blink of an eye. The hail of arrows found their mark at the Ricon, who was at that instant in mid-air, body extended full length, fangs bared, and eyes blazing. He was dead even before he got within striking distance of his intended targets. His head came to rest at the foot of the Goddess.

Nazir pulled the enchanted sword from the dead Ricon. It easily cut through the chains and freed the Goddess, who immediately bent over Jamila. Nazir knew that death was a possibility, but he never thought it would be that of his trusted companion, Jamila. "She saved my life, my lady. And now, she's gone," he said somberly. "It was my fault. I should never have allowed her to accompany me here."

The Goddess Amira looked up at Nazir. "It is not your fault, White Fire. She saved our lives. She was here for that reason. And, she is not dead."

"Not dead, but how…?"

"She was not bitten. Only a small amount of the poison has entered her system from the Ricon's skin. We can save her, but we must hurry."

"What can I do, my lady? Shall I use my staff?"

"Your snakehead staff cannot cure her, White Fire. Only a drop of blood from Haroda has the power to save Jamila from the Ricon's poison. You must find her."

Nazir picked up his snakehead staff, and as he did so, he called out, "Al haber, al asham - Guide me to the witch."

At a full run, he disappeared into the darkness.

CHAPTER 16

"Give Me the Azurat & a Drop of Your Blood, & I May Yet Let You Live"

Nazir did not ask the staff to light the way for him. Somehow, he could feel the presence of the staff inside of him. For all these weeks, he had kept the staff with him – never out of sight or reach. He could feel its presence in his sleep, but now it was different. He realized now that the staff was no longer an object he held in his hand. Now, he and the snakehead staff had become one.

Nazir's eyes now glowed a bright yellow; his skin tingled as the warm air rushed past his skin; he could smell and hear in ways that he never had before– all his senses were alive. It came to him suddenly: he was no longer Nazir, the member of a tribe of wandering goat herders. He was the White Fire. All this time, he thought that although he was the White Fire, the power resided in the snakehead staff. It was true: he had been until now a weak mortal, and had to call upon the power of his snakehead staff for support and protection. But now, he understood: the staff was holding the essence of the White Fire. It waited for the one true person who was pure of spirit, noble heart and courageous in the face of conflict and doubt. The snakehead was an extension of the gods, a channel to them, waiting for him – for the right time to be infused into the heart of a man. Now, he was the true White Fire.

He could see into the darkness. He had no fear, just an overwhelming sense of purpose and determination. He ran as if on air, and maybe he was, as he had no sensation of the ground under his feet. Down and down, he followed the twisted pathway, deeper into Galthoram, running at dizzying speed. In the distance, he saw a small spot of light. It was a mere pinhead, but he knew it was the witch; he could feel it. The spot grew larger, and within seconds, the White Fire exploded into a room. The evil witch saw it. She knew in an instant: this was no longer Nazir, the young boy with the staff. This was the White Fire sent by the gods to defeat her, save the Goddess, and rescue the Azurat stone. The White Fire's terrifying yellow eyes said it all. A rising sense of fear gripped her, but she had little time to quell her fear. The White Fire's voice was different: it was cold, deep and devoid of any emotion.

"Evil witch, it is finished. The Ricon is dead. The Goddess Amira is free. Give me the Azurat and a drop of your blood, and I may let you live."

She tried to regain her composure, but could not overcome her terror. She heard it in his menacing voice, and his yellow eyes grew even brighter. She knew this day would come, the day that she would confront the wrath of Zoltan for her evil deeds, and that day of reckoning was now. She took several steps back, clutching the Azurat stone as the White Fire approached. As he drew closer, he was transformed from his human form into a large serpent that stood more than thirty feet. His head looked part human and part serpent with fierce yellow eyes and fangs. She watched as his skin began to grow scales and turn a mottled black and red. She observed that he resembled... but no, it couldn't be, and yet, she could not shake the thought. The Ricon! This White Fire resembled the Ricon whom he had just killed. In a flash, it came to her as she kept backing away from the approaching beast. In a voice that was shaking now with terror, Haroda said, "That's why the Ricon was here. **He** was the first White Fire. He had done something that so offended the gods that he was condemned forever to Galthoram."

Reading her thoughts, the White Fire spoke, "Yes, witch, the Ricon was the first White Fire sent to save the earth but he failed. He succumbed to conceit and arrogance. He became so drunk with his power, and with his knowledge that he thought himself as great as the gods, indeed as great as Zoltan himself. He rejected the notion that his power was a gift from the gods to be used for the good of mankind. That power only comes from the gods, from Zoltan. I, too, am his instrument – no more, no less. Give me the Azurat and a drop of your blood, and I may yet let you live."

Although trembling with fear, Haroda devised a plan. Yes, it could work, she thought to herself. If the first White Fire could succumb, then why not this one? "So, you are the White Fire, the hand of Zoltan to destroy me. And to what end? After you kill me, do you think that Zoltan will reward you, White Fire? After you have served your purpose, what shall become of you? I know. You shall be returned to be a goatherd with your tribe, scratching out a life for yourself and your mother. You shall eat dust, White

Fire. The gods have no loyalty to humans, no generosity of spirit. They see you as a convenient tool. Why, White Fire, why destroy me when you can have the earth and all its adoring humans at your feet?"

The White Fire kept closing the distance; Haroda kept stepping back. "Witch, you will not corrupt me. One last time: give me the Azurat and a drop of your blood and I may yet let you live."

Haroda knew it was useless. Clutching the Azurat stone that hung around her neck, she summoned a great wall of fire to surround her. She would never part with the stone. It was hers, her reward for a life of sorrow and isolation from the gods. "You shall never have the stone! You will have to kill me first, White Fire," she screamed. The old witch made the wall of flame that leaped up to the ceiling of the cave chamber, almost as tall as the White Fire. He hesitated for a moment. Haroda began to escape, encircled by the ring of fire. She cursed him, the gods and Zoltan for interfering. "This is mine!" she shouted. "No one shall take it from me."

He stepped back, and took in an enormous breath of air. He let it out with a rush that roared like a tornado bearing down on the evil witch. The ball of flame scattered before the enormous wind, and Haroda was thrown to her knees. She covered herself in terror, waiting for the White Fire who loomed over her to strike her dead. In one swift motion, he pulled the Azurat from her neck, pricked her finger with his sharp claws and took a drop of the witch's blood. He backed away for a moment, and stood over her. His snake eyes blazing with anger, he drew back, bared his poisonous fangs, and was about to strike her.

"Wait, White Fire. Have pity," he heard a voice say, emerging from the darkness. "She may deserve death, but show her mercy. That shall be more punishing than a swift death." The Goddess Amira stood at the entrance to the chamber carrying the unconscious Jamila. White Fire's yellow eyes blazed. He roared his reply, "She must die! She has treated the gods with contempt, held you hostage, and destroyed countless human lives, including Jamila. The punishment must be death."

The Goddess said gently, "White Fire, you have accomplished your mission; achieved your destiny. The evil witch is destroyed. The earth and all its people shall be restored. Our father, Zoltan, is the only person who may judge both the living and the dead." With that, the cavern was filled with a thunderous roar – much like a giant waterfall that poured from the top of the cave.

"White Fire. You have done well, my son. Her death serves no purpose. She shall be banished forever in the deepest pit of Galthoram – to the Lake of Eternal Fire. Take her there, White Fire. Put her in chains and leave her. I command you."

Without hesitation, the White Fire wrapped the witch in chains, lifted her emaciated body, and like a snake with its captured prey, slithered into the pit. As she was carried into the dark hole, Haroda alternately screamed, pleaded, and cursed until there was silence. Moments later, the White Fire emerged from the deep. In a blinding flash of light, the serpent was transformed back into a human resembling Nazir. He rushed to Jamila, whose pale and lifeless body was lying on the cold, damp floor of the chamber. He gently placed the drop of blood on her wound; within moments, the young girl's wound had disappeared, and the color of her skin had returned. She slowly, painfully opened her eyes. She searched the face immediately above her. It was Nazir's, but something about him was different. In these last few hours, he had been transformed from the boy with the snakehead stick to something beyond a mere mortal. He had become larger, more powerful, ominous but gentle - all at the same time. "Is it you, White Fire?" she muttered.

"Yes, Jamila, it is I. Welcome back."

He lifted the young woman into his arms. He placed the Azurat in Jamila's hands and said, "You have done so much for me, for the Goddess and for our father, Zoltan. Gesturing toward the Goddess, it should be you to return the stone.

"My lady, I think this belongs to you," Princess Jamila said.

CHAPTER 17

"Thank You"

"Come, my children, let us leave. Our place is with the living," the Goddess Amira said as she put the Azurat necklace over her head. "White Fire, lead us from here."

"My lady, may I beg a favor before we leave?" the White Fire asked.

She knew the reason for his request. "Yes, of course, we must not forget Gaius Fortus. He has done so much for all of us," the Goddess replied.

Instantly, the White Fire vanished. And within a few moments, Gaius Fortus and the White Fire reappeared, walking out of the darkness. The old magician looked haggard. His clothes were in tatters, and his long white hair matted. He bore the wounds of repeated beatings from the old witch. He held on to the White Fire lest he fall. Gently, White Fire led him to the Goddess and Jamila. Upon seeing Amira, the old man fell onto his face.

The Earth Goddess reached down and gently touched the trembling man. "Rise, dear Gaius, my friend. Without you, none of this would have been possible. You gave us the White Fire, rescued Jamila, and, in so doing, saved both the Azurat and me. We owe you a great debt."

The Goddess looked over to White Fire, "Now, White Fire, we are ready." In an instant, a brilliant yellow glow materialized around the White Fire, and engulfed the Goddess, Jamila and Gaius. He raised his hand, and the four were lifted off the ground and carried up from the labyrinths of the cave.

At the very moment, the Goddess emerged from the cave, she closed her eyes and clasped the Stone of Azurat. They could see her lips moving, but there was no sound. She was completely still; nothing stirred – even the wind had stopped. No one spoke.

Amira raised her head to the grey sky, eyes still closed. It seemed as if she were in deep communication with someone or something. Then, she lowered her head, opened her eyes, and took a very long, deep breath, and slowly exhaled. Suddenly, she was surrounded by a halo of deep blue that quickly engulfed White Fire, Jamila and Gaius. The blue light grew larger and larger, and then reached high above them. The sky turned blue, revealing a brilliant sun. She turned slowly to White Fire, Jamila, and Gaius Fortus. Smiling gently, she said simply, "Thank you." And disappeared.

EPILOGUE

In that same instant, the sky above the village of Jabhar turned blue with puffs of white clouds; the wind stirred, and birds began singing. In the village, which had endured years of starvation and pain, the fountains began to gurgle; the plants began to flower, and a gentle wind carried the fragrance of primroses, lilies, marigolds and bougainvillea. The acacias, tamarisks, almond and cherry trees, which for years had been withering under the scorching sun, were restored. In the oases, pools of cool water sprang from parched earth; the desiccated palm and eucalyptus trees began to bloom once again. The earth was being reborn. The Earth Goddess had returned!

Slowly, the villagers emerged from their homes. They could not believe their eyes; they were overjoyed as they witnessed the wonder of Amira's power. They began to celebrate and sing to honor her. "We are saved. Let us erect a statue in her honor," they said. Sha Ram, Jamila's father, smiled to himself and thought, *"They did it! They had conquered the evil Haroda."*

At the same time, the wandering goat herders were the first to notice that the desert earth and sky had changed. They, too, saw the sky turn blue, and the faraway desiccated grasslands turn green again. For the first time in memory, the springs at the oasis were bursting with water. The desert eagle, owl, antelope, and gazelle emerged from their hiding places led by the great wolf, Loganne, the most loyal of Amira's desert creatures. Where there was dust for a crop, suddenly, they saw shoots of barley, peas, lentils and chickpeas. Arosh, the leader of the tribe, convened the meeting of the elders. Pointing to the crop growing in front of his eyes, he exclaimed, "It is a miracle, my brothers. It can only mean that the Earth Goddess has been saved," he said. "Let us give thanks to the gods, and the heroes who have brought us to this day," he said solemnly. He could not see the woman sitting by herself in her small tent with her eyes closed. Lara was smiling. She spoke softly and tenderly, "My son, my beloved child. How you have grown. Yes, they call you the White Fire, but to me, you shall always be my dear Nazir. I shall miss you. Will you come to visit your mother? Perhaps, the White Fire can take a moment to fetch his mother a bucket of water."

Instantly, a large bucket of water appeared in front of her. And from that moment on, and for the remainder of her life, the bucket never emptied for as often as she drained it.

The White Fire waved his arms to create a large ball of light that carried them to Jabhar. The heroic trio was met with cheers from the villagers. They were met at the gate by Sha Ram and the elders. Seeing her father, she ran to him, and threw her arms around him, "Oh, father, I have missed you. The White Fire did it, Father. The witch can no longer harm us, and the great Earth Goddess has been freed. I have so much to tell you."

Sha Ram looked at the White Fire. He could see that the boy who had arrived in the village so long ago resembled Nazir, but he had been transformed in some way that Sha Ram could only feel, but not describe in words. He walked over to the White Fire, and knelt in front of him, "Thank you, White Fire, for returning my daughter to me, and for saving us all."

The White Fire reached down, and lifted the man to his feet, "It is I who thanks you, sir. Were it not for your daughter's bravery and determination, I fear the outcome would have been very different. You have taught her well. You should be proud."

Again, the White Fire spoke. "Sir, I ask nothing of you, but this one favor. It was Gaius Fortus who saved your daughter when she had been captured by Haroda and the Siwa. It was he who guided me in the pursuit of my quest. He has been tortured for years living in the Zunir, the land of the lost souls. He is in need of rest and the comfort of friends. Will you take him in?"

Jamila reached for the old magician's hand. Sha Ram nodded, "It is the least we can do for him and for you."

"And you, White Fire. What of you?" the leader asked. "Surely, you must need rest after your adventures. You must stay with us, and tell us of your deeds."

"Thank you, sir. I would like that very much, but I must go. I have been summoned by the Goddess Amira. The earth is still not safe. There are those who would stand in for Haroda, and continue her evil ways. I know now that my destiny was not this one quest. My mission must continue until all who would defy the gods, and destroy the earth are brought to justice. Perhaps, some day, I shall return this way."

The White Fire leaned forward and gently kissed Jamila on the forehead. She felt a wave of happiness flood over her. "Goodbye, Jamila. Thank you. I shall never forget you." He looked at the old magician. Instantly, the White Fire produced the snakehead staff in his hand. The eyes of the serpent glowed white as the hottest fire. "I am returning this to you, my friend. Use it for good. I shall always be with you – all of you."

And in a flash of blinding light, the White Fire was gone.

About The Author

Philip Antony has drawn on his experiences from his multi-faceted career as a lawyer, business consultant and university professor. He has travelled the world where he was privileged to meet and interact with people of many cultures, which he has woven into all of his stories. He has produced a long line of young adult stories and adult novels in which his rich imagination and international experiences have created a cast of colourful, relatable characters and exciting adventures.

The underlying theme of his stories is the power of love, friendship and compassion that overcome the forces of hatred and division. Although his stories are works of fiction, his novels convey that contemporary message with excitement interspersed with warmth and humour. His work stands in stark contrast to the enmity and divisiveness we read about in our world today.

www.ingramcontent.com/pod-product-compliance
Lightning Source LLC
Chambersburg PA
CBHW070311190726
48291CB00012B/1077